ESCAPE FROM ZOMBIE ISLAND

A ONE WAY OUT NOVEL

DIMENSION Z
PUBLISHING

ESCAPE FROM ZOMBIE ISLAND
(A ONE WAY OUT NOVEL)

FIRST EDITION

This book is a work of fiction. Names, characters, places, and incidents either are the product of the author's imagination or are used fictitiously. Any resemblance to actual persons, living or dead, events, or locales is entirely coincidental.

This work, including all characters, names, and places:

Copyright © 2013 Ray Wallace. All rights reserved.

Cover art: Zach McCain

Interior illustrations: Zach McCain

ISBN-10: 1484829336
ISBN-13: 978-1484829332

No part of this book may be reproduced or transmitted in any form or by any means, electronic or mechanical, including photocopying, recording, or by any information storage and retrieval system, without the written permission of both the publisher and author.

Author's note:

PLEASE READ!

A One Way Out novel, much like the Choose Your Own Adventure books I used to love reading back in elementary school, is not meant to be read straight through. At the end of each chapter, you will be presented with choices. Each of these choices will lead you along a different path through the book. There are many different endings, and as this is a horror story, the vast majority of the endings are rather… unpleasant. Only one path will get you through the story safely. Only one results in your survival.

Best of luck finding the One Way Out.

You're going to need it.

Ray Wallace

Escape from Zombie Island

———————————→ ←———————————

Now this is the life...

Sitting on the beach, you stare at the blue, rolling water stretching into the distance before you. Impending nightfall colors the sky with a rich palette of yellows, reds and oranges as the sun inches ever closer toward the horizon. A cool breeze comes in off the ocean, pushing back the last of the day's lingering heat. The cries of seagulls mix with the steady whisper and crescendo of the waves crashing against the shoreline. You try to remember the last time you've felt this content. It's been a while, certainly. And now you have to wonder why it took such an extreme set of circumstances before you decided to take a break from the job and the daily grind, to find the time to just... *relax*.

Yeah, you could get used to this in a hurry, already have in the three days you've been here. Nothing to do but hang out on the beach, do some sightseeing, enjoy the local food and occasional cocktail, take long naps in the middle of the afternoon and sleep in as late as you wish in the morning. The fact that in four days you have to go back to your regular life... It's a thought you spend little time entertaining. Your tropical getaway will end before long. No point in tainting it with concerns of what might await you back in the real world. The main reason you came here was to put all that stuff behind you. To clear your head. To let all the bad thoughts and feelings drift away... And, certainly, the divorce left you with no shortage of bad feelings. But now the whole sorry mess is behind you. Here you are in this beautiful place, a thousand miles from home, on your own for the first time in over five years, back before the marriage and the year long relationship leading up to it. Alone, yes, but far from lonely. You needed some time to yourself, could use quite a bit more of it, actually, but you'll take what you can get.

With a sigh you get to your feet. The time has come to head back to the hotel, get cleaned up and think about what you want to do for dinner. You could always drop by the hotel bar at some point. Chances are you'll run into some of the other vacationers you've befriended during your stay. You can think of worse ways to spend the evening. Or you could always rent a movie and spend the night in your room.

You grab your towel, shake off as much of the sand as you can, glance around at the two dozen or so people hanging out along this section of beach. The travel agent told you this would be an ideal destination if you didn't want to be bothered by the crowds of the more common tourist traps. Of course, the place's exclusivity had come with a higher price tag. But it had been worth it. The day you arrived you knew this would be the perfect place to unwind.

Turning your back to the ocean, you begin the short walk to the hotel which stands behind a thin line of palm trees, stop in your tracks as a new sound catches your attention. To the north the beach gradually angles back to the east and out of view. Gazing along the coastline in that direction, you see a dark speck in the distance, high above the ground, growing larger and losing altitude as it approaches. The whine of its engine drops in pitch, becomes the choking growl of a machine in distress.

The airplane dips from side to side as the pilot fights for control of the injured craft. People duck instinctively as the plane, trailing a thick plume of smoke, zips by overhead, the letters USAF plainly visible along the undersides of its wings. The aircraft appears to be even smaller than the four seater you flew in while on vacation with your ex-significant other a few years ago. A two seater then. Single engine prop plane. Correction: A *military* two seater, single engine prop plane. Where did it come from? Does the Air Force have a base around here somewhere? On a nearby island, perhaps?

This strange scene goes from bad to worse in an instant when the sputtering engine gives out completely. The plane plummets to the beach, slamming down at the water's edge with a crunching impact, landing gear bent and mangled, nose buried in the sand. Smoke drifts upward from the plane in a thick column as onlookers form a wide half circle around the crash site. A man wearing a tank top with tattoos covering his arms—acting either bravely or stupidly, you're not entirely sure which—approaches the damaged aircraft close enough to look in through the side window. He scrambles backward as the window shatters. Someone inside the plane—the pilot, you imagine—tosses what appears to be a metal cylinder roughly the size of a loaf of bread out through the broken window. The object, leaking a thick, black, misty substance, lands at the feet of the tattooed man. Even from here, you can see the biohazard

Escape from Zombie Island

symbol stenciled on the side of the silver canister. The man coughs as he inhales the black gas. Other onlookers start coughing too as a shift in the breeze carries the mist toward them. From inside the plane the pilot screams, an awful sound reminiscent of the howling of a badly wounded animal. A moment later the cockpit of the aircraft erupts into flame.

People cry out in fear and horror. Someone shouts, "Everybody get back! The plane could explode! Move to a safe distance!" Sound advice and most of those present take it to heart. Several people do not, however, including the man who initially approached the plane. Instead, he and five others drop to the ground and commence thrashing about as though afflicted by seizures.

It's like a scene from a nightmare. You want to do something, anything that might help. At the same time you want to turn and run as fast as your legs will carry you. What good can you do here anyway? You have no sort of emergency or medical training. You'd only get in the way. And since you left your cell phone back at the hotel you can't even call for help. Although, fortunately, distant sirens inform you someone else has made the call. As it's a small island, you can't imagine the emergency personnel taking long to get here.

The people lying on the sand continue thrashing. The plane continues to burn. You close your eyes and shake your head, wishing it all away. But when you open your eyes the awful scene is still there. By now you've seen enough.

You turn and walk across the sand, follow a wooden walkway with ropes for railings past the line of palm trees toward the hotel. The sirens continue to grow louder, closer. As you reach the roundabout in front of the hotel entrance, you hear that howling sound again from the direction of the plane crash. You keep walking, sure you'll hear the awful sound tonight in your dreams.

As you push your way through the glass double doors at the front of the hotel, the cool air of the lobby washes over you. Your sandaled feet pass quietly over the burgundy carpeting as you make your way past the check-in counter toward the pair of elevator doors at the far end of the room. A short time later, you step out of the elevator at the second floor, walk down the hallway to a door marked 203 and use your key card to open it.

Inside, you head straight for the bathroom and turn on the

shower, wanting to clean off the sand and the residue of the saltwater. With any luck it will also help clear away the strange, dreamlike feeling that has settled over you since watching the plane go down.

Afterward, as you dry off then pull on a pair of shorts and a t-shirt, you wonder if you should head back down to the beach, let the police know exactly what happened. But you don't feel up to it. And, besides, it's not like anyone needs your version of events. There were plenty of witnesses, after all.

So now you have to figure out how you want to spend the rest of the evening. Two options come to mind, each of them equally appealing. You could plop down on the couch, stretch out and close your eyes for a few minutes then order room service and a movie. Or you could get out of here, go down to the bar and have a drink, eat at the hotel restaurant instead.

If you decide to lie down for a bit and clear your head, proceed to page 9.

If you think a drink sounds like a better idea then turn to page 13.

Escape from Zombie Island

Power naps have always worked wonders for you in the past. And the room came furnished with one ridiculously comfortable couch. So you lie down and try not to think too much about what you recently went through…

A rumbling sound pulls you out of a dreamless sleep. Disoriented, you sit up and take in your surroundings:

You're in the hotel room, of course. A lamp on a nearby table provides the only light in the room. A counter separates a small kitchen from the main living area and a short hallway leads back to the bedroom. Sliding glass doors offer a view of the patio and the outside world beyond. While you slept, full darkness and a rainstorm settled in. Thunder rumbles once again, this time louder and more insistent.

Getting to your feet, you shake your head trying to clear it of the cobwebs that collected there while you slept.

What time is it anyway?

8:37 PM, according to the digital clock on the entertainment center. You've only been out for half an hour or so. That's good. Any longer and you know from experience falling asleep later on would have been a challenge.

After a quick stretch, you head over to the kitchen, flip a light switch, open the fridge and remove a bottle of orange juice. Leaning against the counter, you open the bottle and quench your thirst.

Damn, that's good.

You realize you haven't eaten since earlier in the afternoon. The evening's agenda will have to include a trip down to the hotel restaurant. Afterward, you can have that drink you contemplated earlier. Considering the day you've had, it might help you sleep a little easier later on.

You lift the bottle to take another long swig of orange juice when a terrible screeching sound reaches you from beyond the room's front door. Startled, the glass slips from your fingers and drops to the tiled floor, shattering and spraying juice and shards of glass in all directions.

"Great," you mutter, staring down at the mess covering the floor.

And then you hear the screeching sound again. It reminds you of something... Yes, the same sort of scream the pilot made before the airplane erupted into flames. Briefly, you wonder if maybe the pilot didn't die after all. Maybe he's out in the hallway right now, covered in burns from head to toe, hardly recognizable as anything human.

"Stop it," you say aloud, trying to cast the ridiculous notion from your mind.

Of course the pilot is dead. No one could have lived through something like that.

Once again, you hear a scream but this time it sounds further away.

What in the world is going on?

Before you realize what you're doing, you leave the kitchen, carefully avoiding any shards of glass with your bare feet. You grab your tennis shoes from where you left them near the front door earlier in the day and pull them on. First things first though... You bring your eye to the peephole, make sure the coast is clear before turning the handle and opening the door. As you take a tentative step out into the hallway, you keep your hand on the door so that it doesn't close behind you.

Down the hall, over near the elevator, you see a young woman in shorts and a bikini top. She has her back to you, head snapping around, long hair flying about wildly, arms extended and hands clawing at the air. If she's not completely out of her mind then she's doing a pretty good impression of someone who is.

"What's the meaning of this?!"

Startled for the second time in as many minutes, you turn around and step away from the door, take in the sight of the old man in the gaudy Hawaiian-style shirt standing there. He looks past you toward the young woman, an angry look on his face.

"Hey, you, enough with all the racket!"

The woman screams.

Actually, you correct yourself, *it's more like a* howl.

Looking back over your shoulder, you see the woman running toward you, eyes wide and crazy looking, mouth stretched in a feral grin. Within seconds she'll be on you with those clawing, grasping hands.

Escape from Zombie Island

Click.

That would be the sound of the hotel room door closing. An image of the key card lying on the countertop near the kitchen sink flashes through your head. And just when you thought this day couldn't get any worse.

"Excuse me," you say as you move past the old man and take off in an all out sprint toward the far end of the hallway. Halfway there you look back in time to see the crazed woman stop in front of the old fellow. She opens her mouth like she's going to scream again but this time a cloud of thick, inky black mist escapes from her mouth, flows directly into the old guy's face. It reminds you of the substance you saw issuing from the metal canister on the beach earlier. The old man cries out in surprise, takes a step back, gets his feet tangled and falls to the floor in a heap.

You approach the end of the hallway. As you've never been down here before, you can only assume there's an emergency exit. If not, you might have to pound on doors and hope someone will let you in.

It turns out you're in luck. The last door on the right is marked with the words "Fire Exit". Without hesitation, you push through into the stairwell beyond. Since you're on the second floor, you can either make your way up to the third floor—and possibly all the way to the rooftop—or down to the hotel's bottom floor.

Initially, it seems like a simple choice: head downstairs, inform the hotel staff about what's going on, have them alert the proper authorities. But then you think about the black gas escaping the girl's mouth. You also think about the tattooed guy on the beach, inhaling the gas from the canister, collapsing and going into convulsions. Had he—and the others who inhaled it—been infected by something in the gas? Had he eventually gotten to his feet and set about spreading the infection by breathing it into the faces of those around him? If so, who knows how many other people have been exposed to the gas at this point. How many other infected maniacs might be waiting downstairs?

Not such a simple choice after all but one that needs to be made quickly. You can't imagine the woman's encounter with the old man slowing her down for very long. In fact, she may be here at any moment.

If you decide to head down to the ground floor, turn to page 17.

If you think you might be better off taking your chances upstairs then turn to page 21.

Escape from Zombie Island

⟶ ⟵

You'd rather not spend the evening alone. Too many disturbing thoughts fill your head. And so you pull on a pair of tennis shoes, grab your key card and exit the room.

You take the elevator down to the lobby and head for the double glass doors leading outside. From there it's a short walk around the building to the pool area. Along the way, you see flashing red and blue lights out toward the ocean. You feel a little better knowing emergency personnel have arrived on the scene.

They've probably already got everything under control.

Even though all but the last of the daylight has faded from the sky, you find several people relaxing around the pool where a rather spirited game of water volleyball is underway. It all has such a feeling of normality to it after the terrible incident you witnessed only a short time ago. Around the far side of the pool, up against the wall of the hotel, stands a bar with a thatched roof over it. You approach the bar and claim an unoccupied stool, search for a familiar face among those gathered there, someone with whom you've socialized before, but you see only strangers.

The bartender walks over, a smile on his face. "What'll you have?"

You want to take your mind off of things, try to get back into vacation mode, so you tell him you'll have something fruity, maybe with an umbrella in it. His smile grows a little wider.

"Coming right up."

Halfway through the drink, you start to relax a little. Another one of these strawberry-coconut concoctions and you'll be just fine. By the time you finish your drink, full darkness has fallen. From somewhere in the distance you hear a rumble of thunder. A nighttime storm may help you relax a little more. If it rolls in soon it will provide a good excuse to head indoors to the restaurant and grab something to eat. You glance back toward the pool and see it has mostly cleared out—the volleyball game has ended. Low music, consisting mostly of ukuleles and steel drums, issues from tiny speakers set into the awning above your head. At this moment, your job and the life you've known for the past several years now feel as though they're a thousand miles away.

That's because they are.

And that's perfectly fine with you.

"Fancy meeting you here."

The stool next to you, previously unoccupied, is no longer empty. Mrs. Rinehart sits there, the elderly widow with the big hair and gaudy earrings you met during the shuttle ride from the airport. She told you she's been vacationing here for the last fifteen years, the first seven of them with her late husband, Alfred. "God rest his soul." No, she didn't find it sad or depressing making the trip without him. Well, maybe that first year she had. But the island called to her, held so many wonderful memories for her, and there was no way Alfred would have wanted her to not make the trip on his account. She had listened and nodded sympathetically as you told her about your divorce, how you'd felt a need to get away from everything for a little while. You'd been surprised to find yourself opening up to a complete stranger like that. Since then, the two of you have run into each other a couple of times and the conversation has flowed smoothly on both occasions.

You tell Mrs. Rinehart—"Please, call me Gladys."—about what you experienced earlier, the terrible thing you witnessed on the beach. As you speak, the first drops of rain fall from the clouds rolling in and blotting out the myriad stars dotting the night sky. Within minutes the drizzle develops into a rather serious downpour. The awning keeps you from getting wet, the raindrops beating upon it loud enough to all but drown out the music. Lightning flashes in the distance followed by the low roar of thunder a few seconds later. Your glass stands empty on the bar in front of you by the time you finish the story. Gladys shakes her head in disbelief.

"Why, that has to be about the most awful thing I've ever heard," she says quite sincerely.

And then somebody screams. No, that isn't quite right, it's more like a *howling* sound that tears out of the nearby darkness.

You turn and look across the swimming pool, the water lit from beneath, surface dappled with the falling rain. Lights mounted on poles illuminate the area. A man enters through the low gate next to a sign with the words "NO DIVING!" on it. As he circles the pool, you recognize him as the guy from the beach with the tattoos, the one who inhaled the gas from the canister then fell down and started

Escape from Zombie Island

convulsing, the same guy you were telling Mrs. Rinehart about only a minute or so earlier. As you watch, he leans his head back and howls once again. Then he makes his way around the pool, directly toward the bar, a rather wild and demented expression on his face. Undoubtedly, the guy is up to no good. And as you've had enough excitement for one evening, it might not be a bad idea to leave before things get even more out of hand.

If you take Gladys by the arm and try to get her out of here before something bad happens, turn to page 25.

If you decide you'd be a lot better off leaving on your own, turn to page 29.

Ray Wallace

Escape from Zombie Island

⟶ ⟵

Decision made, you head downstairs, reach the mid-floor landing where you turn and continue your descent. From above, you hear the door to the second floor open and bang against the wall. Then you hear the sound of the girl's footsteps as she chases after you. At the bottom floor, you grab the door handle just as the girl starts to *howl*... You see her, standing at the top of the stairs, eyes wide and crazed as she looks down at you. Before you can turn the handle and open the door, the girl jumps, propelling herself outward over the remaining flight of stairs, directly toward you.

She lands awkwardly, the sound of something popping in one of her legs plainly audible. Her momentum carries her into you, slams you against the wall, door handle torn from your grasp. You fall to the ground, the girl hovering over you, her mouth opening wide. Struggling against her maniacal strength, you feel a madness of your own take hold at the thought of that black gas washing over you, entering in through your mouth and nose, down into your lungs. Flailing about, you try to dislodge her but to no avail. Any second now the gas will envelope you. Holding your breath will only delay the inevitable. You'll have to breathe at some point. And then what? Will you choke and convulse like the tattooed guy on the beach? Will you go mad like the woman attacking you? Soon enough, it looks like you'll have your answers.

All at once, the girl's body goes slack. She makes a coughing sound but no black breath issues from her mouth. She shakes her head back and forth in a sort of denial. You push her and she falls off of you, rolls onto the floor, lies there on her back staring up at the ceiling. As you climb to your feet you wonder if this might be some strange fighting tactic, some attempt to catch you off guard. The girl kicks her legs somewhat feebly. The wild, crazed look in her eyes vanishes replaced by something else.

Fear.

Pressing your back against the door, you watch as the woman kicks her legs one final time. She lies there perfectly still, this crazed woman who only seconds ago possessed a terrifying energy and strength and a burning need to turn you into something like her.

She's dead.

So it would seem.

Just like that.

With your left foot you prod her shoulder, watch as her head lolls to the side, eyes vacant and unseeing.

Yep, definitely dead.

You don't know what to make of it. You don't know what to make of any of this. What you do know is that you need to get out of here, go to the lobby and tell someone to call the police. You reach for the door handle once again…

And that's when the dead woman moans.

The sound freezes you in place, causes goosebumps to break out along the flesh of your arms. Slowly, the dead woman sits up, all the while staring at you, her eyes vacant and glassy. A trail of spit runs from the corner of her mouth and drips off her chin. She reaches out to you, fingers curled into claws. Then she starts to climb to her feet.

You've seen enough.

You open the door and step through into the hallway, make your way toward the lobby on legs feeling a bit rubbery from what you've witnessed.

A dead woman, come to life…

When you reach the lobby, you see a well dressed young couple standing at the check-in counter. A tall man with the dark complexion of the locals stands behind the counter; he wears a colorful shirt and a nametag informing anyone who reads it his name is Barry. Three sets of eyes turn your way as you tell Barry he needs to call the police and he needs to call them *right now*.

"At first she was screaming. No, *howling*. And she came after me. Then she dropped dead. Except she didn't *stay* dead. Not for long… I mean, you *had* to have seen her. How could she have gotten to the second floor without you seeing her? Did you leave the counter at some point? Take a bathroom break or something?"

You know you're babbling and make an effort to stop. Barry and the couple look at you like you've lost your mind.

After taking a deep breath, you continue in a more reasonable voice: "Can you please call the police?"

The muffled hiss of the rain reaches you through the glass doors leading outside. Thunder roars and dies out as Barry continues to stare at you.

Escape from Zombie Island

"Please," you say.

The sounds of the storm grow louder as the doors swing open. Turning to look, you watch as two men enter the hotel, clothes soaked from the rain. You can tell by the expressions on their faces they're trouble even before one of them opens his mouth and screams. Just then the elevator doors slide open and an elderly man with a cane steps into the lobby. The taller of the two "howlers"—as you've come to think of them—takes off toward the elevator. The second howler bares his teeth and rushes toward the check-in counter where you, Barry, and the young couple await. As the howler nears, the young man courageously steps in front of the woman in an effort to protect her, gets a face full of the black mist for his efforts and starts coughing like he's on the verge of dying from smoke inhalation. The woman shouts his name while Barry makes his way out from behind the counter.

In all the confusion you see an opportunity to escape. There's a simple wooden doorway set into the wall near the elevator. You've seen hotel staff use it on occasion during your stay. It could be an emergency exit although it isn't marked as such. With the howler harassing the old man near the elevator and the dead woman waiting back down the hallway, you really have no urge to go in either of those directions. Of course, you could always use the same doors through which the howlers entered the building only a short while ago. Whatever your decision, you need to make it quick before one of these lunatics decides to infect you with whatever's in that black gas.

If you decide to see what lies beyond the wooden door, turn to page 33.

If instead you head for the glass doors at the hotel entrance, turn to page 35.

Ray Wallace

Escape from Zombie Island

→ ←

If any more of those freaks have made their way into the building, they'll most likely be downstairs.

So you do the logical thing and head in the opposite direction, turn at the mid-floor landing and continue onward to the hotel's third story. From here you can see that the stairwell continues the rest of the way to the roof. *The door up there is sure to be locked, though.* If that's the case then you'd be trapped in here with a crazed woman who wants to infect you with whatever it is that has driven her insane. You reach for the handle of the third floor emergency exit, turn it and pull as a shrieking sound reaches you from the other side.

Another one of those... those howlers.

Below, a door swings open and slams into the wall. The bikini girl's shriek reverberates throughout the stairwell. You push the emergency exit door closed and take off running up toward the roof. When you reach the final landing, you stop and listen to the slapping of feet on the concrete stairs coming your way. Thunder *booms* from outside the metal doorway standing between you and the building's rooftop.

There's no way it will be unlocked.

You grab the door handle.

Only one way to find out.

The handle turns and the door opens.

Well, at least *something* is going your way.

Outside the storm lashes the rooftop like the wrath of some vengeful island deity. It doesn't take long for the rain to soak you through to the skin. The wind swirls and a jagged fork of lightning cuts across the sky. Distracted by this spectacle, you trip over something and stumble, barely avoid sprawling across the fine layer of gravel covering the rooftop. Regaining your balance, you look down and see a red metal box with a handle on it. *A toolbox.* Left here by the same person—maybe a maintenance worker—who also left the door unlocked? Crouching down next to the toolbox, you pop the latch holding it closed before lifting the lid and rummaging through the various tools hiding inside. Your hand closes around something made of metal and very solid feeling. Lightning flashes again allowing you to see it's a wrench about a foot long. Its weight feels good in your hand, reassuring.

You stand and face the open doorway leading back into the hotel, the bright rectangle of light pouring through it like a beacon to sailors long lost at sea. A figure steps into that glowing rectangle, throws back its head and screams. The girl in the bikini top steps out onto the rooftop and walks directly toward you.

Even with the weapon in your hand, you back away. Sure, the wrench offers you some form of protection but the thought of actually using it, of swinging it at this person is not one that you relish.

"Stay back," you say, brandishing the weapon in front of you. Not that you think the words will do any good. "I mean it. Don't come any closer."

And then, quite unexpectedly, the howler stumbles and you think that she, too, has tripped over the toolbox. But, no, she's already stepped past it. And now, as you watch, she falls to a knee, reaches down and places a hand on the roof before going all the way over and lying flat on her back. She cries out and brings her hands up to her throat, rolls back and forth as if being strangled. This goes on for maybe a minute or so before she stops moving.

You stand there, feeling the adrenaline surge through your body, the makeshift weapon in your hand shaking ever so slightly. *What was that all about?* Did your would-be attacker suddenly and inexplicably drop dead in front of you? So it would seem judging by the way she lies on the ground, completely still, eyes open and staring upward into the rain. She doesn't even blink as another bolt of lightning tears across the sky. So, yeah, maybe she is dead. Maybe you won't have to fight her after all.

You approach the woman's motionless form, knowing it's not the smartest thing you've ever done but wanting to make sure she really is dead. As you stand next to her, looking down at her, you lift your foot and give her shoulder a nudge with the tip of your tennis shoe. No reaction. Another nudge, this one with a bit more force. Same result. One more time, hard enough that her head rolls to the side, her face now turned away from you. Still nothing. If she's faking it, she's doing one hell of a job.

Somebody alert the Academy.

Sighing in relief, you stand there letting the rain pelt you as you

Escape from Zombie Island

try to figure out your next move. You need to get inside and out of the storm, for starters. Let somebody know there's a dead body on the roof of the hotel. And after that, you could hide in your room and not come out for anything. Yeah, now there's an idea.

In the rooftop's erratic lighting you see the dead woman's head turn toward you.

No, that's impossible. The dead do not move. A trick of the light, nothing more.

Still, you've developed a sudden and very serious case of the creeps. Yeah, getting back inside the hotel strikes you as a better idea with every passing second. Another fork of lightning cuts across the sky and in that brief flash of illumination you can see you didn't imagine it, the dead girl *has* moved and now she's looking directly toward you, eyes wide and staring, lips pulled back, teeth exposed in a monstrous grin. Startled, you stumble backward and almost lose your grip on the wrench but manage to keep from dropping it. You step back even further as the woman moves into a sitting position. It's hard to be certain but you think you can hear her moaning over the steady patter of the rain. And as if this little development isn't bad enough, an awful shrieking sound erupts from the open doorway. Another *howler*. The one you heard through the door leading to the third floor? Not that it really matters. What does matter is finding another way off this rooftop.

Turning your back on the howler in the doorway and the dead woman struggling to her feet, you take off running across the rooftop, picturing in your mind the grounds surrounding the hotel as you go. Straight ahead—the roundabout in front of the building. Behind you—the hotel's main parking area. To your left—the swimming pool and outdoor bar. And to your right—a wide section of grass leading out to the beach and the ocean beyond.

The crazy idea flashes through your head that you could probably make the jump from the rooftop down to the swimming pool below. But then you catch a glimpse of something jutting upward from the edge of the rooftop ahead and to the right. Casting a glance back over your shoulder, you see the dead woman on her feet, stumbling after you. From behind her the howler screams and gives chase. If you're going to find a way off this roof you'd better do it in a hurry.

You stop when you reach the thing jutting above the edge of the

23

building. It's the top of an access ladder attached to the side of the hotel. You can't help but wonder why, in addition to the stairs, a ladder was thought to be necessary. A way down in case the building caught fire? As good a reason as any, you suppose. If you make it out of here in one piece maybe you'll track down the building designers and ask them personally.

Reaching for the ladder, you know you'll need to be careful. In this weather those metal rungs will be awfully slippery. Half jokingly, you tell yourself you might be better off standing your ground and fighting the approaching howler. Sure, he's obviously one crazy SOB but you're the one with the weapon, right? All you have to do is hit him a good one with the wrench and whatever fight he has in him will disappear in a hurry. Or so you hope.

If you stay put, figuring it's time to fight crazy with a little crazy of your own, turn to page 39.

If instead you decide to use the ladder then proceed to page 45.

Escape from Zombie Island

"Come on, Gladys. Time to go."

"I think you're right," she says, eyes wide as she takes in the sight of the crazed individual circling the swimming pool.

After a quick word to the bartender about the potential trouble headed his way, you lead Gladys down the length of the bar, past the other patrons. Stepping out from beneath the awning, you hurry through the rain over to a glass door set into the wall of the hotel maybe twenty feet away. It leads into the hotel restaurant, a place where you've eaten a few times during your vacation. They serve quality food, the aroma of which hits you as soon as you open the door and usher Gladys inside. Despite the feeling of tension roiling in your gut, the scent reminds you that you haven't eaten since earlier in the afternoon. Getting a table and ordering dinner would be nice right about now. But that's not going to happen. The door closing behind you muffles the sounds of the storm and the beginnings of a scream from outside.

A handsome fellow in a white, long sleeved shirt and a black tie walks over to you. "Table for two?"

Your eyes scan the room, the dozen or so tables with their white tablecloths, most of them occupied by groups of well dressed diners in the act of enjoying their meals. The lights have been turned down low; candles burn at the center of each table giving the place a cozy, intimate feel. Across the room a young man with a classical guitar sits on a stool, long hair pulled back in a ponytail. He strums a song you know you've heard before. At the moment, though, you can't remember what it's called.

"Is there another way out of here?" you ask the man wearing the tie.

"Excuse me?" He wrinkles his brow in confusion.

"Another exit," you say. "There has to be one."

He nods his head. "Through the kitchen. I'm afraid it's for restaurant staff only though. Unless there's an emergency, of course."

Before he even finishes speaking you walk toward the doorway through which you've seen one of the servers recently emerge.

"Over here, Gladys."

She follows and the two of you make your way past the tables.

You're almost at the doorway when you hear a shout from back near the entrance. Turning to look, you see the guy in the tie standing face to face with a middle-aged woman in a red dress soaking wet from the rain. She has her hands on his shoulders, mouth open wide, leaning in toward him. As you watch, a black, mist-like cloud issues from her mouth, enveloping the man's face and head. You've seen that mist before, down on the beach when the tattooed guy took a face full of it himself. But what is it, exactly? Something developed by the military—or so you would guess, considering the plane in which it arrived. For what purpose though? Chemical warfare? Does the gas contain some sort of microbe that takes over the mind of anyone it infects, compelling the person to infect others? Does it drive the person insane in the process? A plausible theory. But you'll be damned if you're going to stick around to test it.

You push through the doorway and into to the kitchen area. Waiters and cooks give you questioning glances as you lead Gladys past the long prep table, through the warmer air next to the oven, past the walk-in cooler toward the closed metal door at the far end of the kitchen. No one tries to stop you, though, as everyone's pretty busy cooking and filling orders. A good thing, too, because even though you don't relish the thought of a confrontation, you're ready to do whatever it takes to get out of here and away from those infected lunatics.

When you reach the door you open it by pushing the release bar attached to it. A dumpster sits nearby. To your left you see the three story bulk of the hotel building; to your right a short expanse of lawn bordered by a stretch of road leading back to the hotel's main parking area. A cement walkway leads over to the road.

While you stand there a scream cuts through the rain and the darkness outside. Actually, the sound resembles more of a *howl* than a scream, the sort of cry a wounded animal would make.

Or an extremely deranged human being.

You think about how you left your cell phone up in your room. It would be nice to be able to call the police. But you've made a habit of leaving the phone behind whenever you've gone out, not wanting to be attached to it, not wanting that connection to the outside world. You're on vacation, after all. The whole idea was to spend a week without thinking about the life waiting for you back home, to put it

Escape from Zombie Island

all on hold for a little while and clear your head. At the moment, though, ditching the cell phone does not look like it's shaping up to be one of your better ideas.

You're about to ask Gladys if she has her phone with her when you see movement outside, a figure heading toward you across the grass from over by the road. Then two more figures appear, running through the downpour.

Who would want to be out traipsing around in this weather?

You get your answer when you heat one of those terrible, inhuman screams.

Those damn howlers *would want to be out in this. That's who.*

You consider making a break for it. Back home you liked to jog most mornings before work, think you can probably outrun any of the maniacs headed your way. But what about Gladys? She's not outrunning anybody. You could close the door, take your chances here inside the restaurant, find a place to hide.

Whatever your decision, you'd better make it quick. Those howlers are going to be here before you know it.

If you tell Gladys to wait here while you try to find help, turn to page 49.

If, on the other hand, you decide to stay where you are and look for a hiding place, proceed to page 53.

Ray Wallace

Escape from Zombie Island

You get to your feet and without a glance toward your drinking companion—doing so would only hasten the guilt you're sure to feel at this abandonment—you step out from under the awning and into the rain. You circle around the deep end of the pool, putting it between you and the tattooed man then head for the gate through which he entered. Halfway there a scream emanates from over near the bar, affirming you've made the right decision in leaving. No telling what mischief the tattooed fellow might have in mind. After the incident with the airplane on the beach, you feel you've already dealt with enough craziness for one evening.

The rain pours down as you push through the gate. With a last look toward the bar and the chaos breaking loose there—it looks like the beginnings of a melee between the tattooed man and several other people—you leave the pool area behind.

A cement walkway leads both left and right, the latter direction taking you back toward the roundabout and the hotel's front entrance. Small lamps glow near the ground to either side of the walkway every ten feet or so. Maybe you should make your way to the hotel lobby, let the guy working the front counter know about what's happening out here, have him call the police. And then you can ride out all this madness up in your room.

Sounds like a plan.

There's only one small problem. When you turn in that direction you see a pair of figures following the walkway directly toward you. If they're in the same state of mind as the tattooed man, you want nothing to do with either one of them.

And so you turn and start to jog the other way, the pool's fence to your left, a thick, well manicured hedgerow to your right. A two lane road runs along the other side of the hedgerow back to the hotel's main parking area. That's where you'll end up if you continue along your current course. And then what? Try to find someone pulling into the lot who has a cell phone, have them call for help? If only you hadn't left your phone up in your room.

Oh, well, spilled milk and all that...

From behind you somebody screams. And then you hear footsteps approaching, following you, chasing you. Running as fast as you can through the wind and the rain, you're glad you decided to throw on a pair of tennis shoes when you came down from the room earlier. Stomping through puddles, you try not to think too much about the forks of lightning splitting the black sky overhead. As you leave the pool area behind, the walkway ahead of you branches off to the left. One path continues onward to the parking lot, the other over to the hotel itself where it ends at a doorway next to a yellow dumpster. You think about trying the door but decide against it. If it's locked you'll only be giving your pursuers a chance to catch you.

Keep moving.

You've managed to stay in pretty good shape these past few years and unless the people chasing you have maintained a similar regimen, they'll fall off soon enough no matter how highly motivated they might be to run you down.

You reach the end of the hedgerow. To your right, a silver car passes by, its tires hissing over the wet asphalt as it makes its way toward the lot where rows of vehicles wait, wet and gleaming beneath the streetlamps bathing the area in illumination from overhead. A backward glance lets you know that your pursuers have not given up the chase. Directly ahead, a palm tree stands to either side of the entrance to the lot. Passing by the closer of the two, you see a bright flash of light. The next thing you know you're lifted into the air, flung away from the tree then slammed down on wet grass and solid, unforgiving ground.

As you lie there on your back, pain consumes the entirety of your body. Pain like nothing you've ever known before. Pain you have never even imagined. You suck in air through your nose, teeth clenched tightly together. Surely the pain has to dissipate at some point. But it doesn't. If anything, it actually seems to intensify. You stare up into the dark sky above, blinking your eyes against the rain. Lightning flickers across the sky but you don't hear the resultant thunder. A realization follows: you can't hear anything at all. There's nothing but silence, complete and absolute.

I've been struck by lightning. And now I'm deaf.

Aside from the blinking of your eyes, you can't move any part of your body.

Two people step into your field of vision, a man with a shaved head and a woman with wet, stringy hair. They look down at you,

Escape from Zombie Island

strange, unreadable expressions on their faces. You try to say something, anything, try to cry out for help but find this normally simple task beyond you. And all the while the pain only worsens, a red tide of agony rising up and up, washing over you, consuming you, firing along every nerve ending in your body until you can't take anymore…

THE END

Ray Wallace

Escape from Zombie Island

⟶ ⟵

You move past the counter over toward the unmarked wooden door. It feels as though you're moving at nightmare speed, like it's taking forever to cross the twenty or so feet to the doorway. But, eventually, you reach your destination.

Please, don't be locked…

The thought flashes through your mind as you reach for the door handle followed by a sense of profound relief when it turns in your hand. As you push the door open, you turn and take in the sight of the mayhem consuming the lobby. Holding what looks like a length of metal pipe—apparently, he had it hidden behind the counter—Barry rushes toward the howler closest to him with what can only be called a look of rage contorting his features. The young man lies on the floor, convulsing uncontrollably. The young woman has her back pressed against the counter, hands held out in front of her, head shaking back and forth in denial. You can't see the second howler or the old man as they have disappeared inside the elevator car. And there, from around the corner leading to the hallway, you see the undead bikini girl step into view, limping badly on her injured leg, teeth bared in a feral snarl.

You step through the doorway, slam the door closed and lock it by pressing a button on the handle. Darkness surrounds you broken only by a thin line of light coming in from underneath the door. Brushing your hand across the wall, you feel a switch and use it to turn on the overhead light. Now you can see you're in a square room maybe twelve feet wide. A desk with a comfortable looking chair behind it takes up most of the space here. Next to the desk a small bookshelf holds a couple dozen books. A vase with a collection of multi-colored flowers sits on top of the bookshelf. An oil painting of a palm tree, a dark sky, and a bright moon adorns the wall opposite the doorway. A cordless phone rests on the desk next to a pile of papers.

An office. It has no windows and only one doorway, the one through which you entered the room. *The only way out of here too.*

Standing there, you tell yourself you have to come up with a course of action, one capable of getting you out of here uninfected and in one piece. Grabbing the cordless phone, you dial 911, hoping

33

the number is universal, that it will work here the same way it does back home. When you hear an electronic ringing from the earpiece you breathe a sigh of relief.

"Come on. Come on..."

You hear the subtle *click* of a connection followed by: "*All lines are currently busy. Please hold for the next available operator...*"

"No, damn it!"

You look toward the door separating you from the madness taking place in the lobby. It dawns on you how easy it would be for someone to force his way into this room. A well placed kick or two and the door would undoubtedly give way. You should probably find a way to reinforce it. *The desk!* All you have to do is move it a few feet, push it up against the door. At least it will slow down anyone trying to come through. Once you do that you'll need to find a weapon of some sort. The two lunatics in the lobby might not even know you're in here but you should take whatever precautions you can. As you circle around the desk, the recorded message repeats itself:

"*All lines are currently busy...*"

And that's when the door crashes open and the maniac who was harassing the old man bursts into the room, a stream of blood running down the right side of his face, eyes wide and brow creased in an expression of animal rage. He moves toward you and for the second time this evening you find yourself in a physical battle with one of these demented individuals. But this one is bigger and stronger. He's on you and has you off balance before you even know it. The phone flies from your hand and you go over backward, falling beneath the weight of your assailant. You see a bright flash of light as the back of your head smacks the corner of the bookshelf. An all consuming darkness rushes in, the type of darkness from which you don't return.

THE END

Escape from Zombie Island

→ ←

You run for the glass doors leading outside into the storm. As you go by, the nearest of the screaming lunatics reaches for you, fingers brushing your arm but you move past him before he can grab hold. Then you're at the doors, pushing your way through, rushing out into the wind and the rain and the roaring of the storm.

You bolt past the lone car parked in front of the hotel, across the roundabout toward the walkway leading out to the beach before you even realize where you're going. The rain lashes you, soaks you through to the skin by the time you reach the other side of the circle. A minor thing to endure, though, if it means putting some distance between you and the madness back at the hotel. You slow your pace a bit as you follow the wooden walkway out toward the beach, not wanting to slip and fall on its slick surface. The leaves and branches of the palm trees to either side of you offer some small protection from the storm's wrath. It's tempting to stay here while you devise a proper course of action but the lightning flickering across the sky urges you to move away from the trees as quickly as possible. So you continue forward, step out onto the wet sands of the beach and into the full force of the storm once again.

Not surprisingly, the area appears to be deserted.

Only an idiot would be out here in this weather.

Despite everything, the thought almost makes you laugh. If you make it out of here alive, you're going to have a hell of a story for everyone back home.

By the veiled glow of the moon and the residual light from the hotel grounds, you gaze upon the dark, rolling mass of the ocean before you. Waves pummel the shore, driven inward by the storm's fury. Further down the beach the wrecked airplane catches your attention, starkly illuminated by a flash of lightning. There it rests, scorched black along most of its length, nose embedded in the sand like the corpse of a once mighty, flying beast. You can't help but wonder why the Air Force has not yet arrived to investigate the downing of one of its craft. Has the weather kept them from doing so? Are they somehow unaware of what's happened here? Do they not care? Or is there a more sinister explanation behind it all?

Mysteries for a warmer, drier environment.

For now, you have to find somewhere safe to hole up and ride out this damned storm.

You notice a vehicle to the left of the airplane, thirty feet or so further inland. *An ambulance.* Dark and forlorn, it has an air of abandonment about it. You can picture the EMT's arriving on the scene, finding themselves in the middle of a scenario rapidly spinning out of control. And what then? Had they been forced to flee on foot for some reason? Or had they been attacked, turned into those things, those *howlers*?

From behind you, somebody screams. Turning to look, you see a figure emerge from the pathway leading back to the hotel.

Yeah, that's right, only an idiot would be out here in this weather. Or a lunatic.

You head further out onto the beach, closer to the shoreline and those crashing waves. Along the way you make out a second figure heading your way from over near the downed aircraft. Then two more emerge from the darkness in the opposite direction. More screaming and the figures close in around you as you walk across the wet sand.

"Get back!" you shout as the foursome draws nearer, always nearer. "Stay away from me!"

But, of course, they don't listen.

You turn and backpedal, try to keep the four of them in your line of sight. The crashing of the waves grows ever louder with each backward step you take. Water swirls up and over your feet, touches your ankles. The person directly in front of you—a woman, her long hair plastered down the sides of her face—lets out an inhuman screeching sound and rushes forward. You stumble back into the water which rises above your knees then up to your waist. The woman lunges at you, grabs you by the shoulders, screaming madly, incoherently the whole time. You try to push her off of you, half crazed with the thought of the woman breathing that black gas into your face. Without warning, a large wave breaks over your head, pulling you from those grasping hands followed by another, even larger wave. You're lifted from the ground, turned end over end in the surrounding blackness, lose all sense of direction, of which way is up or down. All you can do is hope you're not being pulled further out into the ocean, that you'll be able to find your way back to the

Escape from Zombie Island

surface.

A hope that dies when you take in a breath full of water, when you realize you'll never be free of the ocean holding you in its grip.

THE END

Ray Wallace

Escape from Zombie Island

You wipe the rain from your eyes then move toward the middle of the rooftop. If you're going to do this you might as well do it where there's no danger of falling to the ground three stories below. After half a dozen steps, you stop and face the approaching howler.

He rushes through the night like something out of a nightmare. Head shaking randomly, screaming all the while, he draws closer with every stride of his long legs.

What the hell am I doing? you wonder as all the bravado you felt only moments ago, the wild courage that drove you to this confrontation flows out of you. Lifting the wrench in a vaguely threatening manner, you try to keep your hand from shaking.

Too late to back out now.

The howler slows, circles to your left, positioning himself between you and the ladder. There he stops and leans from side to side, distributing his weight back and forth from one foot to the other. His hands come up in front of him, fingers curled into fists, weapons of his own to counter the one you hold. The way he stands gives you the impression he may have had some training as a boxer at some point in his pre-howler existence. Maybe quite a bit of it.

So not only am I going to fight a guy clearly devoid of rational thought but one with skills I couldn't have matched to begin with.

The howler bares his teeth in a wolf-like grin and takes a step toward you.

Aw, screw this.

You reach back and throw the wrench at the guy as hard as you can. It smacks him right between the eyes, sends him staggering then down to a knee.

This would be your cue.

You run toward the doorway leading back into the hotel. Lightning flashes and you see the zombie girl plainly enough, slowly but surely heading in your direction. Plenty of room has opened up between her and the entrance back into the building for you to slip by unmolested. But then a silhouette appears in the doorway, one that screams over the wind and the rain and charges out onto the rooftop.

So much for that idea.

You alter your course, run across the rooftop to the side opposite that with the ladder.

Maybe there's another way down over here.

You can only hope.

It turns out not to be the case, though.

Before long you run out of room, find yourself standing at the edge of the rooftop, looking down at the hotel bar below and the swimming pool just beyond it. The place looks deserted although you see a few people run by outside the fence marking the perimeter of the pool area.

"Not good," you say under your breath, mentally kicking yourself for not using the ladder while you had the chance. A scream catches your attention, forces you to look over your shoulder toward the dark figure approaching from the doorway. Another scream lets you know the howler you hit with the wrench hasn't forgotten about you either.

"Not good at all."

You return your gaze to the swimming pool, try to convince yourself that with a running start you could clear the bar and hit the water. With a pair of howlers closing in, however, you're not going to be able to get a running start, not even a short one. Is it possible to leap far enough from a standing position? It seems highly unlikely.

I'd rather jump and not make it than stay here and be turned into one of those—

One of the howlers tackles you from behind and sends you flying through the air off the edge of the rooftop. The problem is you don't fly nearly far enough. No, mostly what you do is plummet straight down toward the thatched roof of the bar which, as it turns out, does very little to slow your descent. You tear right through it, slam down through the shelves with all the bottles and glasses lined up across them and onto the cement floor. Fortunately, the howler managed to wrap his arms around you and hold on to you the whole way down. While you fell, you turned so the howler ended up underneath you, taking most of the impact with the roof and the floor. Still, you don't walk away unscathed. For a while, you don't walk away at all.

Rain pours down through the rather sizable hole in the ceiling above you. Rolling off the body of the howler, shards of glass cut

Escape from Zombie Island

you in various places along your arms and legs. These injuries, however, pale in comparison to those already sustained. Sucking in air, you cry out at the pain erupting along your left side, so intense you nearly black out. It's safe to assume you have a few broken ribs. A broken wrist too, judging by the fact you can't move your left hand. And the way your right heel collided with the floor leaves little doubt the bone in there has been similarly damaged.

Minutes pass before you manage to push yourself into a kneeling position, your back against the wall where the shelves of bottles once stood. In all this time the howler has not moved at all nor uttered a sound. *Out cold or dead.* You'd bet on dead considering how much worse his injuries have to be than yours.

It's dark in here, quiet except for the rain and the occasional rumble of thunder. Even with the bad weather, you know people would have normally gathered here. It takes more than a little rain to keep people separated from their drinks. You have little problem imagining what might have caused the area's desertion. A gathering of revelers would have undoubtedly attracted the attention of a howler or two.

A flash of light, sharp and blinding, interrupts your thoughts. You raise a hand to block it from your eyes, hiss at the pain caused by the sudden movement.

"My God," says a woman's voice from behind the light. "What happened to you?" Followed by: "Oh, sorry."

The beam of light swings up toward the ceiling, through the hole there.

"You have got to be kidding me."

"I wish I was," you manage to say.

Footsteps approach, crunching broken glass.

"You need a doctor," the woman tells you, voice filled with concern. The flashlight beam pans down to the floor. "Oh, no." There's a moment of silence. "I don't know if a doctor can help him."

You look at the howler lying in front of you. Eyes open, he stares unblinking into the falling rain. A sizable puddle of blood has spread outward from beneath his head like a crimson halo.

"He was beyond help anyway."

"What do you mean?" asks the woman.

"He was... howler."

41

"You mean one of those screamers? Those maniacs?"

You nod your head.

"They showed up here," the woman tells you, "attacked people, chased everyone else off. I hid in the restaurant and tried to call emergency services on my cell phone but all I got was a recording saying all the lines were busy. When the power went out I found a flashlight below the cash register, came outside to see what was going on, if things had settled down. And that's when I found you in here."

You summon the strength for two more words: "Help... me..."

"Of course."

She crouches down and you lean forward, away from the wall while she places an arm around your waist.

"On three then. One... Two... *Three*."

Standing, you cry out against the combined agony of your injuries. It's a slow process, leaving the interior of the bar, an equally slow trek around to the stools lining the front of it where you sit down. An awning above your head protects you from the rain. The lighting is a little better out here and for the first time you get a good look at the woman helping you. She's close to middle age with shoulder length brown hair pulled back behind her ears. Long pants, a dark blouse, and a low pair of heels make up her outfit. For the first time you also see the steak knife she holds in the same hand with the flashlight.

As far as weapons go, it's better than nothing, you suppose.

"We're never going to make it anywhere like this," the woman tells you. "So I'm going to get my car and then I can take you to the hospital." She hands you the knife. "Just in case." You take it from her. "Okay, then. I'll be right back."

With that she turns and walks briskly into the storm, around the swimming pool and over to the gate set into the fence along the other side. Then she disappears from view leaving you alone with your thoughts and the dead howler lying in the bar behind you.

The minutes crawl by, more than enough time for the woman to have made it to the parking lot behind the hotel—where you assume she went to get her car—and return. You're getting antsy sitting here. A howler or some wandering dead person could show up at any moment. And where would that leave you, sitting here badly injured

Escape from Zombie Island

with nothing but a steak knife to protect yourself? As much as you don't like the idea of getting up and moving around, you know you can't sit here much longer.

But what if she shows up after I leave?

To paraphrase The Clash and their classic song: Should you stay or should you go now? Tough decision. After all, it could be a matter of life or death. *Your* life or *your* death.

If you tell yourself you should wait a few more minutes for the woman to show up, turn to page 57.

If you think it's a bad idea to stick around here any longer then proceed to page 63.

Ray Wallace

Escape from Zombie Island

$\longrightarrow \quad \longleftarrow$

You stick the wrench in the pocket of your shorts, turn around and place your foot on the top rung of the ladder. The howler continues to run directly toward you with the dead girl trailing at a much slower pace. As a blast of thunder causes the metal of the ladder to vibrate, you begin your descent to the ground below.

This is a really bad idea, you tell yourself as the wind and the rain conspire to pull you free of the ladder. You're several rungs down when a piercing shriek causes you to look upward. And there's the howler, staring at you from the edge of the rooftop.

Concentrate.

Returning your attention to the ladder, you continue down as quickly and carefully as you can. Along the way you notice something that momentarily confuses you then gives you an anxious feeling: a second ladder behind the one you're climbing. You only hope it doesn't mean what you think it means.

Halfway down the side of the building you reach out with your left foot, ready to place it on the next rung only to discover there is no next rung. Looking down, you see nothing but empty space beneath you. The bottom half of the ladder has been raised and, you would assume, locked into place.

"Wonderful," you mutter, glancing upward to see the howler now descending the ladder too. Left with no alternatives, you carefully lower yourself and hang by your hands from the bottom rung. Then you let go.

When you hit the ground, you slip on the wet grass and sit down hard, look up in time to see the howler lose his grip and fall from the ladder. He lands badly, slamming down on his side with his arm tucked underneath him. Something inside of him audibly snaps and you wince as he lies there whimpering and gasping for breath. You feel pretty certain about one thing: he won't be trying to breathe any of that black gas into your face anytime soon.

You get to your feet, feeling a touch of pity for the injured howler lying on the ground in front of you.

Better him than me.

You head off into the storm, try to decide on your next course of action. Nowhere seems safe now. As you approach the parking lot behind the hotel you wish you had a car so you could drive out of here, away from all this madness. But there had been no need for a rental since you could walk or take a cab anywhere you wanted to go. It would be nice to call a cab company right now, have them come and get you. That's not going to happen though. Even if you had your cell phone you can only imagine how that conversation would go:

Yeah, I'm aware several maniacs are on the loose in the area but if you could send one of your drivers over to pick me up, well, that would be great... Hello?... Hello?...

Speaking of maniacs...

As if on cue, a tall figure lurches out from between a couple of parked cars at the edge of the lot, lets loose with a scream and charges right at you. Without thinking, you pull the wrench from your pocket. When the lanky fellow gets close enough you take a swing at his face and connect, snapping his head sideways. With that swing, all the tension and fear you've felt since the airplane crashed on the beach wells up inside of you, morphs into something else entirely, a black rage the likes of which you've never experienced before. You just wanted to relax, to put all the stress of the past several months behind you. And now this? You lash out again and again, send the howler to his knees on the blacktop then onto his back, a sizable gash spilling blood down the side of his face. Standing over him, you hold the wrench out in front of you, ready to inflict more damage if the guy makes any unexpected moves. Looks like you did a pretty good number on him though. He lies there staring up at you, looking rather dazed and bewildered.

"That's right, stay down," you tell him, trying to sound a lot tougher than you actually feel. Your heart pounds in your chest. The rage coursing through your body begins to subside. You take a deep breath, trying to calm your nerves.

"Hold it right there!"

Startled, you turn and squint into the headlights of a car you didn't even know was there.

Must have snuck up on me while I was dealing out that ass kicking.

Blue and white lights flash on the roof of the vehicle. A man wearing a dark rain coat with a gun in his hand stands next to the

Escape from Zombie Island

open driver's side door. He points the gun in your direction.

"Police! Drop the weapon and put your hands in the air!"

Damn. You really don't want to drop the wrench. Even injured, you have a feeling the howler at your feet still represents a serious threat. And God only knows how many others like him are out there. They might arrive on the scene at any moment. Maybe the cop will understand if you try to explain the situation to him, let him know you are definitely not the problem here. Although the way he's standing there pointing that gun at you makes you think he may not be in much of a listening mood.

If you think you should hold onto the wrench and state your case, turn to page 61.

If you decide you should do as you're told, proceed to page 65.

Ray Wallace

Escape from Zombie Island

→ ←

"I'm going for help," you tell Gladys. "Close the door as soon as I get outside."

With that you step through the doorway. With each passing second the howlers draw nearer, ever nearer. Looking back, you see Gladys standing in the open doorway, watching you.

"Close it!" you tell her.

She nods her head, a grim expression on her face. "Be careful," she says then pushes the door closed.

Lightning cuts across the sky overhead. Thunder booms. The rain continues to fall with nothing but bad intentions.

You run.

Your path angles to the right, across the lawn toward the two lane roadway that merges with the parking lot at the rear of the hotel. Palm trees stand to either side of the lot's entrance, leaves whipping about in the swirling winds of the storm. Multiple screams erupt from the howlers as some of them break from the pack and give chase. At the edge of the road you turn and follow it away from the parking lot toward the front of the hotel. To your right a tall hedgerow blocks the view of the pool area where you and Gladys had been enjoying one another's company only minutes earlier.

You run as fast as you can across the pavement, the heavy rain threatening to blind you at times. Wiping your eyes and looking back over your shoulder, you see one of the howlers, a thin man in his early twenties, coming after you with everything he's got. He's about fifteen feet behind you and even though you've always stayed in pretty good shape, you fear he'll catch up with you sooner rather than later. And what then?

He'll try to give you a heavy dose of the black breath.

The very thought of it spurs you to run a little faster.

When you reach the end of the hedgerow, two people step into the street from the direction of the hotel. One of them, a woman, leans her head back and *howls* into the torrent of the storm. Without breaking stride you veer around them, move closer to the middle of the road. A sports car speeding by almost hits you, the blaring of its horn warning you to get out of the way. Still running, you wave your hands over your head and shout at the departing vehicle:

49

"Stop! Please, stop!"

You can't believe your eyes when you see the red glow of the car's brake lights as it pulls over to the side of the road. Approaching the vehicle, you circle around to the passenger side door which springs open when you get there. Throwing yourself inside, you reach out to pull the door closed, cry out when a hand clamps down on your forearm and tries to pull you free of the car.

"Go!" you tell the driver. He stomps the accelerator. The hand, however, does not immediately let go of your arm. The person—the howler—it belongs to ends up getting dragged a good twenty feet along the wet pavement before losing his grip and tumbling out of sight, a parting scream cut off as you finally manage to pull the door closed.

Leaning back in your seat, you take long, deep breaths. Your heart feels like it's trying to jump out of your chest. The car picks up speed over the gleaming black road cutting through the landscape before you. Glancing to your left you see that the driver is a young man in a button-down, short-sleeved shirt and a pair of jeans, dark hair matted to his head from the rain. He's got a small scar near the corner of his mouth, visible in the green glow coming off the dashboard. He meets your gaze and offers a tight smile.

"Well, this has turned into an eventful evening."

The road curves steadily to the left, further inland, away from the ocean. Directly ahead you see an intersection with a flashing red light.

"What the hell is wrong with those people?" asks the driver—your savior—as he slows the car and glides up to the intersection.

"Some sort of infection." You tell him about the airplane crashing on the beach earlier. The metal canister... The black gas...

"Air Force, huh?" He shakes his head in disbelief. "You'd think they'd be more careful with... Well, whatever was in that canister."

You can't argue with that. "Where you headed anyway?" you ask.

He shrugs. "I was walking over to the hotel bar when I heard a bunch of shouting. By the time I got there, all hell was breaking loose. Looked like a small riot. Then some guy came around from the front of the hotel, started screaming and chasing after me. By then I guess I was pretty freaked out so I ran over to the parking lot,

Escape from Zombie Island

decided to get out of there."

The rearview mirror gleams with approaching headlights.

"Name's Trent, by the way." He holds his hand out to you.

Taking it, you give it a brief shake, tell him your name in return, thank him for stopping and saving your ass.

"Not a problem," he tells you. "By the way, I'm thinking we should go by the police station and report what we saw. I have no idea where it's at, though. I flew in this morning, rented a car and spent the day at the hotel. I've got relatives flying in tomorrow. Thought I'd wait for them to show up before I did any sightseeing."

"I don't know where it is either," you tell him. If you had your cell phone you could call information and find out. Trent has his phone but it's dead and he doesn't have the charger with him. Yeah, that seems to be the way things are going this evening.

"Got any sort of a hunch?" asks Trent. He gives a nod toward the intersection where you can either turn left or right or continue forward.

If you tell Trent to go straight through the intersection, turn to page 73.

If you decide to go left, proceed to page 77.

If you think you should go right, turn to page 81.

51

Ray Wallace

Escape from Zombie Island

⟶ ⟵

After thinking about it for a few moments, you decide against going out there and trying to outrun a group of those maniacs. Plus, you can't leave Gladys behind to fend for herself. You close the door, listen as the lock clicks into place, hoping it's enough to thwart the howlers coming your way, at least for a little while. Screaming can be heard through the doorway leading back to the dining area. It sounds like all hell breaking loose out there. Making your way through that chaos doesn't seem like a great idea either. So you're going to have to hide in here, wait until things have calmed down a bit and try to make a break for it then.

You lead Gladys over to the front of the walk-in cooler, grab the handle and give it a pull then usher Gladys inside. A single bulb beneath a clear plastic cover provides plenty of light to take in these new, frigid surroundings. The entire area is about a dozen feet long by maybe half that wide. Metal shelves stacked with plastic bins of food, boxes of produce and jars of vegetables line either side of the cooler. You don't see any good hiding places. Your only hope now is that none of the maniacs invading the restaurant will decide to look in here.

Gladys retreats to the back of the cooler and leans against the wall, arms crossed in front of her, eyes wide with fear. Already you feel the cold set in, not surprising given the fact that you're a bit wet from the storm and dressed for much warmer surroundings. You wrap your arms around yourself, attempting to hold in as much body heat as possible.

"What now?" asks Gladys, the expression on her face letting you know she doesn't have much faith in whatever answer you're going to give her.

"Now we wait."

You look around for something you can use as a weapon. Maybe somebody left a knife or some other dangerous cooking utensil on one of the shelves. There's nothing, though. If any howlers find you in here you'll have to resort to some hand to hand combat, a scenario you do not relish—no pun intended.

Gladys has her cell phone out, trying to get some reception within the bunker-like confines of the cooler, without success. You pass the next several minutes in silence, listening to the muffled shouting coming through the cooler's walls. Shouting that suddenly gets louder accompanied by an animal-like howling that you've already come to know all too well. Attached to the inside of the door is a metal plunger with a green, plastic cap on its end which, when pushed, will allow the door to open. You reach out and grip it with both hands, hoping in this way you can hold the door closed against anyone trying to get in here.

Moments later, someone pulls on the handle from outside. Tightening your fingers around the circle of plastic, you place a foot against the wall next to the door and brace for the next pull. For maybe half a minute, you manage to keep the door closed. And then the plastic cap pops free in your hands. Off balance, you stumble backward and fall sprawling across the cold, hard floor.

The door flies open and a man stands there, wet from the storm, eyes wide and teeth bared in the sort of grin that can only be described as psychotic. He leaps forward and lands on top of you, pinning your shoulders to the floor. He opens his mouth and breathes into your face. A black cloud envelopes you, causes the world around you to go dim. As much as you don't want to you end up inhaling that inky blackness down into your throat and lungs. All the while Gladys shouts for the man to stop but he doesn't listen—no big surprise there. You start to choke and thrash about, feel as though you can't breathe. Your assailant stands up, leaves you lying on the floor as an unbearable, searing pain spreads throughout your body.

I'm going to die. The thought echoes repeatedly through your mind.

But you don't die.

The pain lessens. You can breathe again. Your limbs come back under your control.

Sitting up, you realize you're alone in the walk-in cooler. You know there were other people in here at some point but, right now, that doesn't really matter. What does matter is spreading the infection that has taken up residence inside your body. That and nothing else.

As you exit the walk-in cooler, three people go running by in rapid succession. Howling like animals, they disappear through the exit door which now hangs open. You follow them without

Escape from Zombie Island

hesitation, take off running through the rain and the darkness. You find yourself howling too, much like a wolf calling to others of its kind. With the infection spurring your actions and clouding your thoughts, language fails you and this primal form of expression is all you have left.

Eventually, you make your way to a street lined with bars and nightclubs. Despite the weather, plenty of people wander about, some beneath raised umbrellas, others rushing from one awning or alcove to the next. You join a group of howlers and manage to infect three people by breathing the black gas into their unsuspecting faces. The fun ends, though, when an off duty police officer shoots you in the back then shoots you again as you turn around and lunge toward him, screaming all the while. A third shot puts you down for good.

Apparently, it's true what they say about all good things coming to an end.

THE END

Ray Wallace

Escape from Zombie Island

———————————→ ←———————————

Just a few more minutes. If she's not back by then it'll be time to go.

And so you sit there with the rain beating on the awning above your head. Wind whistles through the hole in the roof behind you. You hear a woman shouting, "No! No! Stay away!" from somewhere outside the pool area. An indistinguishable figure hurries along the sidewalk beyond the fence followed by two others. Hard to say if it's the same woman you're waiting on. You can only hope not.

A few more minutes…

You feel a touch of dread at the very thought of standing up because you know how much it's going to hurt. It hurts plenty right now without moving at all. You'll have to find a way to deal with it, though.

To your right, a man steps into view from beyond the edge of the bar, walking hurriedly with his head down, as if with a purpose. There's something about the way he moves, the muttering sound you can hear him making over the steady hiss of the rain… Confirming your suspicions, he raises his head and screams, snapping his head back and forth like a rabid dog.

Don't look over here… Don't look over here…

Somehow, miraculously, he does not at look you. Instead, he moves through the rain over to the gate, pulls it open and passes through.

The breath you didn't even know you were holding escapes in a rush causing you to wince and place your uninjured hand on top of your damaged ribs. A minute passes while you try to calm your frazzled nerves. By then you decide you've waited long enough.

Slowly, deliberately, you climb off the stool and onto your good foot. You suck in air through your teeth as you place the other foot down with as much care as possible.

There, that wasn't so bad.

Despite the pain, a low chuckle escapes you.

Yeah, who am I kidding?

Now all you have to do is walk.

And go where, exactly? The hotel lobby?

As far as finding help, it's probably your best bet. With the way you feel, however, you may as well try to walk all the way across the island while you're at it.

I can't stay here though.

You take a step with your right foot then your injured left, do what you can to put as much weight as possible on the ball of the foot. Still, you find yourself groaning in pain.

Another step.

Someone enters through the gate. A woman. Definitely not the woman you've been waiting on. Her long hair hangs in strands down her face. The left sleeve of her t-shirt is missing. She wears a skirt that hangs to her knees, the skin covering her right shin mostly torn away. At first she doesn't seem to notice you but then her gaze locks onto you and she raises her hands, reaching out to you. When she moves a little closer you can see the vacant look in her eyes.

"Wonderful."

You grip the steak knife in your hand more tightly even though you know any sort of physical confrontation—given your current condition—will more than likely not end in your favor. And so you move away from the zombie, one excruciating step at a time. With the third step you lose your footing on the wet concrete, stumble and come down hard on your bad heel. A spike of agony causes your leg to buckle. You fall to your knees, nearly topple all the way to the ground while trying to keep from using your damaged left hand. Kneeling there near the deep end of the pool, you breathe deeply, summoning the strength to rise and walk again. By the time you climb to your feet, the zombie has closed the distance between the two of you. Before you can move away from her, she wraps her arms around your neck and buries her teeth in your shoulder. Crying out, you try to lunge away from her. The move throws you both off balance and the next thing you know you plunge head first into the pool.

With the zombie's weight attached to your back, you sink straight to the bottom, losing possession of the steak knife along the way. All the while the dead woman keeps biting and biting... It turns out she's stronger than you would have expected. With only one good hand, you find it impossible to free yourself from her grasp. And the fact that she's underwater doesn't seem to bother her at all.

Escape from Zombie Island

Maybe it has something to do with being dead and not having to breathe. You, on the other hand… At least you can stop worrying about having to walk around on that bad foot of yours.

THE END

Ray Wallace

Escape from Zombie Island

There's no way you're dropping the wrench, not with the howler lying at your feet, not after all you've been through.

"Officer, let me explain." You have to raise your voice to be heard over the storm. "You might not be aware—"

"I said drop the weapon!" Obviously, this isn't going the way you hoped it would. "Now!"

You take a step in his direction, away from the howler, hands raised above your head, wrench still gripped tightly in your fist. You need to make him understand you're not the threat here, that the man lying on the ground is the person he should be concerned about, along with the untold number of others just like him out there in the rainy darkness. Not to mention the dead people who've decided they don't want to stay completely dead anymore.

"If you'll allow me to—"

There's a sharp cracking sound followed by an explosion of pain in your right shoulder, like someone has stabbed you with a knife coated in acid. The bullet's impact knocks you back a step and spins you in a half circle before you fall to the pavement not five feet from the howler. You roll onto your back, gaze up toward the dark veil of clouds obscuring the stars above.

"Oh, damn." The words come out of your mouth as you wonder how much worse this night can actually get. Hard to top getting shot, you suppose. Although with that howler lying nearby...

You sit up, the pain in your shoulder causing you to groan involuntarily. You need to move, can't risk getting infected by the howler. The approaching police officer draws your attention. He still has the gun aimed in your direction. When he's about ten feet from you he stops and speaks into a walkie-talkie, his voice too low for you to understand. Then he tells you not to move, to stay where you are, that more police officers and an ambulance are on the way.

"But, officer, please, you've got to—"

Something slams into your injured shoulder. The pain of your injury explodes, makes the world go gray and fuzzy around you. When everything snaps back into focus, you find yourself lying on the pavement once again. As for the howler... He kneels over you, eyes wild as he looks down at you, hand raised in a fist ready to strike you again. His mouth opens wide and you wait for the black gas to pour down over your face…

The *crack* of a gunshot. The howler flinches, a scream escaping him as he climbs to his feet.

"Do not move! Stay where you are!" shouts the police officer.

Thunder roars and you try to push away from the howler. The movement only intensifies the pain, however, and you realize as a darkness wells up inside of you that you've found a way to escape this madness after all.

You pass out.

Then:

Screaming. No. *Howling.*

Rising up out of the darkness, a cold wave of panic washes over you.

Got to get out of here…

You can't move though. Opening your eyes, you turn your head from side to side, discover that you're on your back, tied down to a firm but comfortable surface. Some sort of mask covers your mouth and nose. Next to you sits a young man dressed in a blue shirt and black pants. He leans in and tells you to relax, that everything's fine.

"You've been shot. We're taking you to a local hospital. Your injuries are not life threatening. Everything is going to be all right."

The howling you hear is nothing more than the sound of a wailing siren. You're in an ambulance. How long you've been unconscious, you have no way of knowing. A few minutes? Half an hour?

You shout from behind your mask that everything is *not* going to be all right. The *howlers...* And those other things, the *dead* things. The *zombies...*

"They could be anywhere by now!"

You feel a sharp stinging sensation in your arm and the EMT tells you once again to relax. "Don't worry, you're in good hands. In practically no time you'll be as good as new."

The fear and the panic start to fade. The darkness wells up inside of you again. And, just as before, it pulls you under...

Proceed to page 69.

Escape from Zombie Island

———————————→ ←———————————

I need to get out of here…

You stand up, hissing through clenched teeth as your various injuries protest the move. Before you can change your mind and sit back down, you start to walk, trying to keep as much weight as possible off the heel of your left foot. You step out from beneath the awning and into the rain, start to circle the pool and head for the gate.

And after that?

The hotel lobby seems like the most logical place to go. Hopefully you can find someone who can offer you some assistance there. Although, right about now, it seems so impossibly far away.

Put one foot in front of the other…

Halfway to the gate you hear the one sound you definitely did not want to hear. Screaming. No, *howling*. It comes from behind you. Turning enough to look back over your shoulder, you watch as a man emerges from the doorway leading into the restaurant's dark interior. From here, even in this poor lighting, you can see the grin that cuts its way across his face. For some reason, the expression does nothing to alleviate the sudden anxiety you feel.

Well, this is gonna suck.

You make a dash for the gate. Actually, it's more of a hobbling half run. Spears of agony shoot their way up from your foot, through your leg and seemingly throughout the whole of your body. You keep moving, though, the very thought of the man exhaling the black gas into your face driving you onward. Looks like it's true what they say about fear being the ultimate motivator.

When you reach the gate you stop and pull it open. As you step through the howler slams into you in much the same way as the guy on the roof of the hotel. Once again, you fall. This time, however, it's a much shorter distance to the ground. Still, it's far enough to cause further injury, especially when you land on the steak knife, burying the blade into your torso, up under those fractured ribs of yours.

63

Talk about a rough night! Good thing it's over, right? Hard to imagine it would have gotten any better from here.

THE END

Escape from Zombie Island

→ ←

"Okay, okay," you tell the police officer as you toss the wrench to the ground.

He approaches, gun pointed at you the entire time. "Turn around and face the other way. Put your hands behind your back."

You do as your told, feel cold metal encircling your wrists. The howler lies there in the rain, seemingly disoriented from the smack to the head you gave him with the wrench.

But for how much longer?

You want to put some distance between yourself and the fallen maniac. A palpable sense of relief washes over you when the cop leads you over to the cruiser. He pats you down to make sure you're not carrying any other weapons. Then he opens the rear door of the car, lightly pushes down on your head and guides you inside. When he closes the door, you try to make yourself as comfortable as possible. After that you can only watch through the metal cage separating the front seat from the back and the rain spattered windshield beyond as the police officer walks away.

It really comes as no surprise when you see the howler sit up and then climb to his feet. The police officer stops in his tracks, shouts something you can't make out over the drumming of the rain on the roof of the car. Without warning, the howler screams and charges directly toward the cop who lifts his arm, shouting all the while. The howler doesn't stop and so the cop opens fire. *Pop! Pop! Pop!* From inside the car's sealed interior, it sounds like a toy gun's pale imitation of an actual firearm. The first shot appears to have about the same effect as a toy gun too. The second shot, however, stops the howler in his tracks. And the third one sends him back down to the pavement.

The officer stands there for a few seconds, not moving. Then he approaches the fallen howler, kneels down next to him for maybe half a minute before returning to the car. Along the way, he reaches into his raincoat, pulls out a walkie-talkie and speaks into it. Behind him, lightning cuts across the sky. Then he's at the driver's side door, opening it and getting into the car.

"Oh, man," you hear him say.

Looking into the rearview mirror, you see the reflection of his eyes gazing back at you. No mistaking the look of disbelief there. You wonder if this is the first time he's ever had to shoot someone.

The guy can't be more than twenty-five years old. Probably new to the force.

It had probably seemed like a fairly simple gig, patrolling the streets of an island paradise. And it probably had been until tonight, until a certain plane crash landed on the beach, releasing the nightmare contained within that metal canister.

The car's radio crackles to life and the officer breaks eye contact, reaches for the transmitter hanging from the dash, thumbs down the button and says all of two words: "This is—"

Something slams up against the car, rocking it back and forth.

"What the hell?!" he shouts.

There's another impact, this time from the opposite side of the car. Through the windows you see two people standing in the rain, looking in at you. One of them shakes her head back and forth, screaming all the while. Then, as you watch, they both back up, readying themselves for another run at the cruiser, to use it like some sort of tackling dummy.

"Um, officer..."

Three more people arrive on the scene, one of them holding what looks like a chunk of asphalt in his hand. You hear more screaming from outside the vehicle. And then the howlers charge the car *en masse*.

The cop puts the car in gear as two of the howlers slam into it and that chunk of asphalt goes bouncing off the windshield.

Thank God for plexiglass.

A woman dives onto the hood of the car, reaching for one of the windshield wipers swishing back and forth. The cop hits the gas, tires momentarily spinning on the wet surface of the parking lot before catching and sending the car forward. He turns in time to keep from running over the wounded—or possibly dead—howler lying on the asphalt. The car picks up speed before the cop stomps the brake pedal. The move presses you up against the metal grid of the cage; the woman on the hood slides off and disappears from sight. You're thrown back onto the seat as the car accelerates again, u-turns around the end of a row of parked cars and races toward the parking lot's exit, a palm tree standing to either side. Leaving the lot,

Escape from Zombie Island

the car speeds through the rain and the darkness along the road bordering the hotel's property.

Grabbing the radio transmitter again, the cop describes an attack by "a group of deranged individuals" in a voice sounding more than a little bit shaky. He also says something about "bringing in a perp." Considering everything that's occurred, you find it hard to believe he still plans to go through with taking you to the station and charging you with a crime. You let him know this as he slows the car and turns through an intersection.

"Be quiet back there," he tells you. "Unless you want to end up in more trouble than you're already in."

"I think we're all going to end up there anyway."

"Be quiet. I mean it."

You do as you're told, realizing it's pointless to say anything more. Sitting back, you try to relax and enjoy the ride as much as possible. The police car cruises down a long stretch of road where you assume the power has been knocked out by the storm. The houses and buildings here stand dark and traffic lights blink yellow. Eventually, all that changes as you turn onto a street where rows of bars, nightclubs and restaurants garishly illuminate the way. A block or so past the last of these fine establishments, the car pulls over and parks before a rather nondescript gray building. The cop gets out and opens the back door, helps you out of the vehicle as thunder erupts and the rain pelts you once again. He leads you along a cement walkway up to a set of wide, stone steps. Then he ushers you through a glass doorway and into the lobby of the local police station.

Proceed to page 93.

Ray Wallace

Escape from Zombie Island

You come out of it slowly. Blinking your eyes against the light, you try to remember what happened to you, how you ended up here—wherever "here" is exactly.

Several minutes go by and it comes to you in bits and pieces. The plane crashing on the beach... The crazed girl in the hall outside your hotel room... The escape from the roof of the hotel... Attacking the howler with a wrench... Getting shot by the police officer... The ambulance ride...

Looking around, you see you're in a small, spartan room with white walls. A vase filled with flowers sits atop a small table pushed against one of the walls. An open doorway leads to a hallway beyond. Next to the bed upon which you lie, a plastic bag containing a clear liquid hangs from a thin metal stand. A tube runs down from the bag and into your left arm where it's held in place with an adhesive bandage. To your right you see a window with a set of half-drawn blinds hanging over it. Rain runs down the glass in tiny rivulets. Outside, the world is dark.

So you're in a hospital somewhere, lying beneath a thin blanket covering you to your chest. A digital clock on the nightstand next to the bed informs you of the time: 1:32 AM. Several hours have passed since the policeman decided to put you down with a bullet. A brief feeling of panic flutters in your chest. God only knows how many of those damned howlers could be out there, rampaging across the island by now. Not to mention the zombies... You can only hope the proper authorities have taken control of the situation.

And who would that be, exactly? The police?

You have a feeling they might be a tad bit undermanned to handle something like this.

The military then?

You almost laugh at that.

Yeah, the same people responsible for triggering this whole mess in the first place.

You know the island has a fairly sizable city near its center. It would only make sense to place a hospital near that city. Which would currently place *you* near that city.

A major population center with lots of potential hosts for the

69

howler infection.

You need to get out of here, head for somewhere less crowded, somewhere you might be able to find a way off this island without being turned into one of those screaming maniacs.

Throwing aside the blanket, you swing your legs over the side of the bed. A terrible ache settles into your shoulder. Groaning against the pain, you get to your feet, stand there a bit unsteadily as the room goes in and out of focus a few times. You take in long, deep breaths until everything settles back into place once again. When it does, you realize you're dressed in a hospital gown, the kind that hangs down to the knees and ties in the back. And you're not wearing much of anything else. If you're going to make your way out of the hospital and into the storm you're going to have to find some more suitable clothing, that's for sure.

First things first though.

You peel the bandage from your arm and then, gritting your teeth against the pain, pull the plastic IV tube free in one quick motion. As blood wells up from the opening in your skin, you press the bandage back into place.

Damn, if this isn't the worst night ever.

Aside from the one leading out to the hallway, the room has two other doorways, both of them closed. One of them opens on a tiny bathroom where you relieve yourself, wash your hands and your face at the sink before drinking a few paper cups worth of water. Behind the other doorway hides a closet. Inside you find clean cotton t-shirts and matching pants on hangers along with comfortable looking slippers on the floor. Changing outfits, the room around you goes blurry again. You know a doctor would never clear you to leave the hospital in this condition.

Desperate times and all that.

Once the dizzy spell passes, you cross the room and enter the hallway.

Walking across the gleaming linoleum floor, you glance into the rooms you pass, see patients sleeping in a few of them, the hissing and beeping of various pieces of medical equipment the only sounds you hear. Where are the nurses? The doctors? The orderlies? Shouldn't there be somebody making the rounds, checking on the patients? Reaching the end of the hallway, you raise a slightly

Escape from Zombie Island

trembling hand, press the button that summons the elevator car. You don't have to wait long for it to arrive.

When the doors open a woman rushes out toward you, eyes wide and wild looking. Alarmed, you take a couple steps back. She doesn't attack you, though, doesn't scream incoherently or try to breathe that black mist into your face. Instead, she tells you to go back, *go back...*

"It's a nightmare down there! A group of people came in. They looked badly injured, like they'd been in a car accident or something. One of the doctors walked over and tried to speak with them. Before he even said three words they grabbed him, surrounded him. And then they..." She stopped and shook her head in disbelief. "They tore at him with their hands. Then they started to... started to *eat* him."

The woman wears a light blue nurse's uniform.

"You can't go down there," she tells you. "We're safer up here. We need to find a place to hide, a place where they can't get us. I've got my cell phone. We'll barricade ourselves in, call the police and wait for them to show up."

If nurse's plan sounds like a good one, turn to page 85.

If you still want to try to leave the hospital then proceed to page 89.

71

Ray Wallace

Escape from Zombie Island

→ ←

"Straight ahead," you tell him, seeing no reason to turn here. He nods his head then gives the car some gas, pulls through the intersection. You see no lights burning within any of the buildings and houses here.

The power must be out.

You wonder when the storm might end. As of right now, it shows no signs of letting up anytime soon.

Considering the weather, Trent's going a little faster than you like, not that you can blame him. You're anxious to find help too. A few cars go by in the opposite direction. After that, you and Trent have the road to yourselves, a long stretch with no buildings of any kind along either side.

The rain increases its assault on the vehicle. You can't see much of anything more than twenty feet beyond the windshield. The car ascends a small rise in the road before heading down the other side. You think about telling Trent to slow down, that it's not going to do either of you any good if he loses control of the vehicle. Just then a man materializes out of the rain and the darkness, standing in the middle of the road. Trent curses and stomps the brake pedal causing the car to go into a long skid over the wet pavement. For a fraction of a second, you lock eyes with the man in the road. He stares right at you, eyes wide in the glare of the headlights, a grin on his face. Then the front end of the car plows into the guy sending him over the hood and up against the windshield hard enough to crack it. He flies up and over the roof as the car continues to slide across the blacktop, slowly turning so it faces back the other way, eventually drifting into the grass and dirt at the side of the road where it stops.

Trent curses, slams his hand against the steering wheel over and over again. You reach out and grab him by the arm, shout his name, force him to look at you.

"We have to go see."

"But what if it's one of those..." He leaves the thought unfinished.

"We still have to go see."

A moment passes before he reluctantly nods his head.

"If he is one of them," you tell him, "I doubt he's going to pose

73

much of a threat."

Another nod, this one with a bit more certainty. "There's a flashlight in the glove box."

Trent engages the emergency brake and turns on the hazards, leaves the engine running and the headlights on as the two of you exit the vehicle and start walking. It's a good thirty or forty yards to where the guy lies sprawled across the blacktop. When you reach him you see that he's alive. But he's not looking so good. His left leg below the knee has been twisted in a way it certainly wasn't meant to be twisted. His right arm appears to be seriously injured too. His nose now points to one side of his face, a stream of blood pouring out of it. The guy makes a wheezing sound, his mouth opening and closing like he's trying to say something.

Trent curses again as he stands there looking down at the guy, at the extent of his injuries. Then he kneels down next to him, like he wants to help but has no idea how.

"Careful," you tell him.

"Look at him," says Trent, shaking his head. "Even if he is one of them, he doesn't deserve—"

The guy reaches up with his uninjured left arm and grabs Trent by the shirt. With a tortured scream, he pulls Trent—caught off guard and off balance by the move—down on top of him. The screaming stops and you can see the black gas drifting out of the howler's mouth directly into Trent's face. You back away as Trent starts making these awful, choking noises. There's nothing you can do now but turn and run, head back to the car and get out of here before you suffer the same fate.

Good thing he didn't turn off the car and take the keys with him.

You open the driver's side door and get in, sit there trying to figure out what you should do.

Stick to the plan, find the police station.

You put the car in gear and pull onto the road, approach the rise where the accident occurred, look over to where Trent and the howler lie on the wet pavement. You want to stop and do something for this man you hardly know. After all, he stopped to help you out when he didn't have to.

This is different though. A lot different.

There's nothing you can do. As bad as it makes you feel you

Escape from Zombie Island

have to keep going. So you give the car some more gas, wanting to get back to the intersection as quickly as possible.

Without warning, headlights appear at the top of the rise. The other vehicle, a four wheel drive pickup truck, swerves around where Trent lies in the road, over toward the center line. The next thing you know the truck crosses into your lane and slams into Trent's rental car head-on. Unfortunately, you're not wearing your seatbelt. Add to that a bit of bad luck when the airbag, for some reason, doesn't deploy.

Oh, well, that's the way it goes sometimes.

THE END

Ray Wallace

Escape from Zombie Island

→ ←

"Left," you say, knowing this will take you further inland. It strikes you as the most logical choice.

Trent nods. "Left it is then."

As the two of you cruise along, the storm gains strength. Rain lashes the car and wind buffets it from side to side. The road widens to four lanes for a stretch and several vehicles pass you heading the other way. A few minutes later, you reach the outskirts of the island's main city.

"Can't think of a better place to put a police station," you say.

Trent agrees and follows the signs taking you downtown. The city's main strip is lined with bars, nightclubs and restaurants, streetlamps and neon lighting the way. People hurry along the sidewalks, most of them holding umbrellas or jackets over their heads.

Good to see the howler outbreak hasn't kept everyone from going out and partying.

Apparently, word of the spreading infection hasn't reached this part of the island yet.

"Anything around here look like a police station to you?" asks Trent.

"Not so far."

Trent pulls up to an intersection and stops. A group of four people wander out into the middle of the crossroads, none of them carrying umbrellas, seemingly oblivious to the rain. One of them, a man, tilts his head back and screams; the other three join in.

"Oh, great," says Trent as two of the howlers break off from the pack and head your way.

From the right, another car approaches the intersection. The driver beeps his horn, trying to get the howlers to move out of the way. Instead, all four of them swarm the vehicle, screaming and punching at the windows as the driver leans on the horn.

"Let's go," you say.

Trent drives through the intersection. Halfway along the next block you tell him to slow down.

"Look! There!"

Two police cruisers sit in front of a low, squat building next to a side road. Trent pulls in behind the nearest car and kills the engine. You get out and hurry through the rain toward the glass doors at the front of the building.

Once inside, you stand there looking around, dripping rainwater on the linoleum floor. At the far side of the room, an overweight fellow with a receding hairline dressed in the blue and black uniform of the local police stands behind a long counter. The wall to your right has a closed metal door set into it. Behind the counter you see another doorway, this one open, offering a partial view of a room beyond with desks in it.

As you cross the room, the cop looks up from the open manila folder in his hands, sets it on the countertop and asks, "Is there something I can help you with?" According to the metal nametag pinned to his chest, his name is Sergeant Nelson.

"Yes, Sergeant, there most certainly is." You relay to him, as succinctly as possible, the events of the evening beginning with the plane crash landing on the beach. The officer listens as you speak, not interrupting, nodding his head on occasion. When you finish he stands there without saying anything, like he's thinking about what you told him. From outside you hear a roar of thunder.

"Well?" you eventually say.

The officer shrugs. "We're on it."

You blink, not sure you've heard him correctly.

"You're... on it?"

"Yes, we're always on it. Our best officers are out there right now, maintaining order. It's what they get paid to do and they do it well, I assure you of that."

"I'm not sure you understand—"

He holds up a hand, silencing you. "I understand perfectly well. And, like I said, we're on it."

Trent steps forward. "And what does that mean, exactly?"

The cop's expression darkens. Before he can reply, you hear a commotion from behind you. Turning around, you see a woman in her mid-thirties dressed in a dark shirt and a pair of jeans enter through the station's front doors. She has her hands cuffed in front of her. A young male officer follows closely behind. They're both soaked from the rain. The officer listens as the woman explains how the police have much bigger concerns than her right about now.

Escape from Zombie Island

"Call somebody," she says. "Call in the damn army! Because you're gonna need them. By the look of what's going on out there, you already do. This thing's gonna spread, believe me. It already *is* spreading! Another hour, two at the most, and the whole town will be overrun. Hell, half the damn island could be overrun by then..."

"Yeah, yeah, yeah," says the officer as he guides the woman over to the counter.

"What you got, Cody?" asks Sergeant Nelson.

"Public disturbance. Might be a dee-and-dee."

"I'm not drunk!" says the woman.

"Really?" says the young officer. "Tell it to the judge."

The two of them make their way to the end of the counter where there's a gap between it and the wall. Shortly thereafter, they disappear through the open doorway leading into the other room.

You spend a few more minutes trying to convince Sergeant Nelson of the severity of the situation taking place outside. When he says "We're on it" for the third time you have to restrain yourself from reaching across the counter and strangling him.

"This is a waste of time," says Trent. "Let's get out of here."

As much as you hate to admit it, you have to agree with him. What now though? This was the plan, after all, getting to the police station, finding help. Where do you go from here?

"Thanks for nothing," you can't resist saying.

Just then you hear shouting from the other room. A moment later the woman appears in the doorway, except now she's not wearing any handcuffs and she has a gun in her hand which she points at Sergeant Nelson's head.

"Get down! Now! Face down on the floor!"

He doesn't need to be told twice.

The woman hops up and sits on the counter, swings her legs around and drops down in front of you. She raises the gun and points it in your direction.

"Move out of the way!"

Behind you, the sound of the storm grows louder. And that's when the screaming begins. Turning your head, you see a group of people entering the building. Five of them altogether. Crazed looking people who charge across the room directly toward you. Trent grabs you by the arm and pulls you to the side as the woman opens fire, the gunshots loud enough to hurt your ears in the lobby's enclosed space.

Two of the howlers go down immediately followed by two more. The fifth one takes two shots to the chest and one to the knee before he finally joins the others on the floor, howling like an animal with its leg caught in a trap.

The woman walks over to you, asks if you want to make it through this night alive.

It takes you a moment to respond. "Of course I do."

"Then follow me," she says and walks past the bodies over to the entranceway.

If you do as she suggests and follow the woman out into the night, turn to page 97.

If you stay where you are, deciding the woman might be as dangerous as anything else on the island then turn to page 101.

Escape from Zombie Island

→ ←

You shrug and tell him to take a right. "If it doesn't work out we can always turn around."

Trent doesn't bother with the blinker as he turns the wheel and gives the car some gas. The road here gradually curves back and forth, rises and falls with the undulation of the land. Houses with big yards sit to either side of the road, the space between them increasing until, eventually, they disappear altogether. Now you see nothing but grassland and palm trees, the leaves and branches of the latter whipping about in the wind and the rain. Through the passenger side window the ocean comes into view, a rolling black mass merging with the horizon. Trent falls silent for a while as he concentrates on the road, windshield wipers on high, the car's headlights cutting through the darkness.

After five minutes of this, you decide you're definitely headed in the wrong direction.

We're not going to find a police station out here, that's for sure. Should've taken a left at the light, headed further inland.

On a positive note, though, you've been moving further away from the site of the plane crash, ground zero for the howler outbreak.

Less chance of getting infected out here. Especially if we keep moving.

The thought brings you some comfort and you relax for the first time since being chased by those screaming maniacs. Each second that goes by takes you further from any chance of infection.

Although...

It's not inconceivable that the disease—bug, virus, whatever you want to call it—may be spreading faster than you realize. Which would mean the howlers have covered more ground than you realize. After all, the ones you encountered did seem pretty motivated when it came to finding new carriers of the black gas. By that line of thinking, the howlers could be pretty much anywhere at all, waiting for some unsuspecting travelers to come along.

All of a sudden, you don't feel quite so relaxed anymore.

"Trent, I think we should—"

Something slams into the windshield, causing a web of cracks to appear across its length. The car drifts to the right, into the grass at the side of the road. Trent whips the wheel to the left, oversteering and sending the car hydroplaning across the wet pavement. You instinctively place your hands against the dashboard, bracing for impact, lose all sense of direction as the world outside the car goes spinning by. It all ends with a *crunch*. You take the brunt of the impact with your shoulder and the right side of your head.

Everything goes black...

Until:

Screaming.

You also hear a repetitive dinging sound.

Opening your eyes, you blink a few times against the car's interior light.

To your right, you see something that defies your ability to immediately comprehend. It looks like a tree trunk, right there where the passenger side window used to be. Your seatbelt holds you in place, trapping you against the door which has been bent inward. Looking to your left, you see a guy—his name begins with a T, you think, but you're not entirely sure—sitting there looking back at you, eyes wide with fear as several sets of hands reach in through the open door next to him, grabbing him by the arms and shoulders. His mouth hangs opens and you think he's the one screaming. But then you realize the terrible sound comes from outside the car. The noise hurts your head and you want to tell everyone to shut up but you can't find the energy to raise your voice above the din. And so you sit there and watch as the guy in the driver's seat—*Thomas? Terry?*—gets pulled from the car and disappears into the darkness beyond the open door.

None of it feels real to you. Easy enough to imagine you're still unconscious and dreaming the whole thing. A pleasant thought, to be sure, but you know better. You're in shock. This feeling of disassociation from everything going on around you is the mind's way of dealing with an extremely stressful and traumatic situation. You've been in a car accident, after all. Smashed up against a tree. The entire right side of your body feels numb. Paralyzed. In contrast, you feel something warm and wet flowing down the side of your face. You reach up and touch it with your left hand. The tips of your fingers come away red.

Blood.

Escape from Zombie Island

The sight of it transfixes you. When something tugs at your arm you hardly even notice. A face leans into your field of vision, a madman's face that opens its mouth and exhales a cloud of black mist. You have no choice but to breathe it in.

Darkness descends, a darkness from which you know you will never emerge. You succumb to your injuries before the infection has a chance to set in. Really, it's the best you could have hoped for given the circumstances.

THE END

Ray Wallace

Escape from Zombie Island

The nurse's suggestion tempts you, especially considering the way you feel physically. If you fell over right now it would hardly surprise you. Not to mention the constant pain in your shoulder, the dull ache that has set its teeth deep into the muscle there. You close your eyes against a bout of dizziness until the feeling passes.

"Good idea," you say once the floor settles into place underneath you once again. "We'll barricade ourselves in. Wait for the police to arrive."

"This way then."

The two of you walk to the last room at the end of the corridor. Inside, a comatose man lies on a bed with an IV in his arm and a tube down his throat. A nearby respirator hisses a steady rhythm accompanied by the beeping of a heart monitor. The nurse leads you to a chair next to a table laden with cards and vases filled with flowers. Glancing at one of the cards you see a scribbled sentiment: "Get well soon, Henry." Looking at Henry—eyes closed and circled with black rings, head wrapped in bandages—you have to wonder if there's any chance of that happening.

Cell phone in hand, the nurse heads for the door, tells you she'll be back in a few minutes.

"Gonna try to find a signal."

While she's gone, you sit there and listen to the noises made by the various pieces of medical equipment and the rain as it taps at the window like nervous fingers on a desktop. You think about what the nurse told you, how the zombies attacked the doctor and started eating him.

The living dead.

You wonder how smart they might be. Smart enough to use an elevator, to come up here in search of fresh meat to satisfy their hunger?

Despite these grim thoughts, you find it increasingly difficult to keep your eyes open. Your head feels as though a great weight has settled into it. How nice would it be to let your eyelids slip shut and doze off for a little while…

"Damn. Nothing." Startled, you look up and see the nurse standing in front of you, staring at her phone, brow creased with

85

concern. "Now doesn't that figure…"

Yeah, you suppose it does. All of a sudden hanging out here and waiting for the troops to arrive doesn't seem like such a great idea. Because if there's no way to contact those troops…

"How are you feeling?" the nurse asks you.

A shrug. You wince at the flare of pain in your shoulder. "I've been better."

"Can you stand?"

You tell her you can and prove it by climbing to your feet.

"The door doesn't have a lock," says the nurse. "Do you think you can help me move this dresser?"

She indicates a long, waist-high piece of furniture near one of the walls.

"I think I can manage that."

You take a few steps toward the dresser before you notice the little old lady sitting at the opposite side of the table, previously obscured by the collection of flowers standing between the two of you.

"Hello there," she says with a friendly smile, like she doesn't have a care in the world.

"Uh, hello."

"This is Mrs. Kelly," says the nurse. "She's been staying in the room across the hall. I brought her over while you were nodding off. Thought she'd be safer here with us."

Together, you and the nurse manage to slide the dresser across the floor and move it into place against the door, preventing access from the hallway beyond. Job completed, you place your hands on top of the dresser and watch as tiny black dots jump back and forth in front of your eyes. The nurse disappears through a doorway you assume leads to a bathroom, reappears a few moments later holding some pills in one hand and a paper cup filled with water in the other.

"Here, this should help with any… discomfort… you might be feeling."

Discomfort. Yeah, that's one way of putting it.

After swallowing the pills, you settle back into the chair and wait for the medication to work its magic. Closing your eyes, you listen as the nurse asks Mrs. Kelly if she needs anything. It isn't long before you drift off once again…

Escape from Zombie Island

"I need your help!"

The voice sounds familiar but you can't place it immediately.

"Hurry!"

Then you see the nurse by the door, bent over and pushing against the dresser.

You stand up then half stumble over to the dresser, add your weight to it, brace it against whatever's trying to push its way in through the doorway. You hear a scream from the other side of the door, a certain type of scream you've heard before.

Howler.

Something slams against the outside of the door. Again. Each time the dresser slides back an inch or two and each time you find it impossible to push it back to its previous position, as if some great weight presses against it. Slowly, inexorably, the door opens further and further, the gap ever widening. A hand reaches in followed by two more. Finally, the door opens wide enough for the first zombie to come through: a woman with a lost, vacant look in her eyes, her mouth caked with gore. Moaning, she moves toward you.

Outside, from the hallway, a howler screams.

Then the door opens even further and zombies pour into the room. They surround Mrs. Kelly and take her down. Next they move on to Henry who sleeps through the attack, blissfully unaware of the horrors inflicted upon his body. You and the nurse circle around the bed, can do nothing but watch the carnage as teeth and hands go about their grisly business, ripping and tearing at the man's flesh, at all the slippery things hiding underneath.

You look around for something you can use to smash the window, desperate for any means of escape. But it's too late for that. So you try to fight off the zombies but there are too many of them. The painkillers don't help a whole lot with what happens next. Yeah, it's a messy, terrible ordeal but it's fairly quick. As the world around you goes black, you hear the nurse start to scream.

So much for that wonderful plan of hers.

THE END

Ray Wallace

Escape from Zombie Island

———————————→ ←———————————

You tell the nurse the last thing you want is to be trapped in this building, waiting for help that may never arrive.

"No, I think I'll take my chances outside."

You walk past the nurse and into the elevator car.

"Good luck," she says as the doors slide shut.

You press a button embossed with the letter L and the car descends. The digital display above the door informs you of each floor you pass along the way. The car stops when it reaches the lobby. When the door opens you see, first hand, the nurse was correct: it *is* madness down here.

The place is literally crawling with zombies. There has to be more than a dozen of them, the majority on their hands and knees, feeding, tearing the flesh and muscle and other, less easily identifiable pieces from a trio of bodies. The white scraps of a doctor's outfit cling to what's left of one of the bodies. The zombies partake in what can only be described as a feeding frenzy, moaning and growling as they use their teeth to tear at the chunks of raw meat in their hands, moving from one body to the next, driven by what appears to be an insatiable appetite for human flesh.

You stand there, gazing in awe and horror upon this grisly scene. So far, none of the zombies have taken an interest in you.

Only because they haven't noticed me yet.

If you're going to make a move it has to be now. And so, as the doors begin to close, you summon every ounce of courage you have within you and step out of the elevator car.

Looking around, you see a reception desk to your right. To your left a doorway leads into the hospital gift shop. And there, maybe thirty feet in front of you, transparent doors offer a view of the rain and the darkness outside.

Eyes on the prize.

You run, following a narrow pathway through the middle of the zombie gathering. *Now* you've got their attention. One of them reaches toward you, slaps at you with a bloody hand leaving a nasty red stain on your clean, white pants.

Halfway there.

You step on a section of flooring slick with gore, lose your

89

footing and almost go down. Somehow, though, you manage to stay upright, to keep moving forward.

Nothing can stop me.

Near the end of the pathway, one of the kneeling, undead creatures lunges out in front of you, sprawling across the floor, doing what it can to block your way. You've come this far though. *No turning back now.* Before you can even try to talk yourself out of it, you take two more steps toward the zombie and you *leap...*

Ever so briefly, the zombie manages to grab your slipper, throwing you off balance. Extending your arms to break your fall, you go crashing to the hard linoleum floor. Pain explodes in your shoulder and you feel like you might black out. But you don't. Instead, you rise up onto your hands and knees then climb to your feet, convinced all the while that several of those cold, dead hands are about to grab you, pull you away from the doors and hold you down while you're slowly torn to pieces.

Looking back, you see some of the zombies have stood and started to move toward you, awkwardly, like marionettes with broken strings.

Time to go.

The entrance doors slide open automatically. You step through, welcoming the feel of the rain on your skin, happy to have made it out of the hospital alive.

You follow a cement walkway out to the edge of a four lane road next to the hospital grounds. Across the street you see a long, low building with several doors set into the front of it, each bearing the name of a different business. A couple of cars go by as you stand there contemplating your next move. Fatigue threatens to cloud your thoughts. The rain—along with the pain in your shoulder—helps to clear your mind. You have to stay focused until you find somewhere safe from the monsters terrorizing the island. Hard to believe so little time has passed since you were relaxing on the beach, thinking about what you might have for dinner. Talk about life throwing you a curve ball... You're still in the game though. And with any luck you could still win this thing. All you have to do is find a way off the island which means you have to keep moving.

A distant scream has you turning and looking off to the right where you expect to see a group of howlers. For now, though, the

Escape from Zombie Island

street lies empty in that direction. The sound of gunshots draws your attention back the other way. They too reach you from a distance, not an immediate concern but one that should be taken into consideration.

Right or left, those are the choices. Toward the screaming or the gunshots. To say that neither option appeals to you would be a bit of an understatement.

Then again, why would things get any easier now?

If decide to go right, turn to page 113.

If you choose to go left instead then proceed to page 117.

Ray Wallace

Escape from Zombie Island

Once inside the station, you have your fingerprints, photograph and pertinent information—name, home address, etc.—taken by an older, overweight fellow with a receding hairline. Afterward, you're led down a hallway to a holding cell, a twenty by twenty room with a row of bars running floor to ceiling in place of a front wall. Amazingly, the cell is empty. Looks like you're the only one who's been arrested so far this evening. The night is young, though. You should have your share of cell mates by morning if you haven't gotten out of here by then.

Trying not to let recent events get you down, you tell yourself at least you're safe from all the madness taking place outside in the storm. In fact, you can't imagine a safer place on the entire island than in here, locked in this cage. Small consolation, really, for what you've been through but for now you'll take it.

You sit down on a bench attached to the rear wall of the cell and try to relax. As time passes, a deepening fatigue presses down on you—no doubt stress related—and you decide that, hey, since you're all alone in here you might as well get comfortable. So you lie on your back on the bench, knees bent and hands folded over your stomach. You just need to close your eyes for a minute or two, fight off the headache threatening to set in.

And before you know it…

You doze off. When you come out of it and open your eyes you have no idea how much time has passed. A few minutes? An hour? Longer?

A clock would be nice right about now.

Getting to your feet, you walk over and grab a pair of the metal bars preventing you from stepping out into the hallway beyond. A muted rumble lets you know the storm continues outside. Besides that, you can't hear much of anything, strange since you're pretty certain it was some sort of noise—something other than the storm—that woke you to begin with. You stand there telling yourself it was nothing, a dream maybe, something imagined.

A wordless shout reaches you from down the hallway.

Nothing imaginary about that.

"Hello?" you say. When there's no reply you try again, a bit louder this time: "Hello!"

Two gunshots in rapid succession: *Blam! Blam!* Lots of shouting now. A string of curse words. More gunfire. Shoes clapping against the linoleum of the hallway. A police officer runs past your cell. You don't recognize him. His shirt sleeve is torn, blood trailing down his arm.

"What's going on?" you shout at him. He doesn't even slow down. A second later he's out of sight and you hear a door opening and slamming shut.

The sight of the fleeing, bleeding officer unsettles you, to put it mildly. Something bad is going down and you're trapped in here. In your mind's eye you see howlers spreading out across the island, infecting anyone and everyone they come across. Has a mob of those deranged individuals attacked the police station? *A very good possibility.* Although why haven't you heard the trademark screaming sound they like to make? Instead you hear more gunshots. More shouting. The sound of breaking glass. Then: Moaning. The *thump-drag* of someone with an injured leg coming down the hallway. The patter of liquid dripping onto the linoleum.

A woman walks into view noticeably favoring her left leg. She wears a leather boot on her right foot; the left is bare. A gray skirt, badly torn along one side, hangs to her knees and dark stains cover the front of her blouse. What really gets your attention, though, is the sight of the decapitated head she holds in her hands. As you watch she bites into it, tears off a piece of its face with her teeth, moaning all the while. Blood drips from the stump of a neck and onto the floor.

Revolted, you back away from the bars of your cell.

The woman stops walking, lowers the severed head and looks your way, face matted with gore and blood, a chunk of skin dangling from her lips as she chews and chews and chews... She lets the head fall to the floor with a wet *thunk* then approaches the cell, presses herself up against the bars and reaches out to you with her bloody hands, fingers curled into claws. You keep moving back until you bump into the bench and sit down, the strength flowing out of your legs. All you can do is watch as the woman stands there, reaching through the bars, moaning all the while. There's an emptiness in her eyes, much different than the madness you saw burning in each of

Escape from Zombie Island

the howlers' eyes earlier in the evening. You think of the girl in the bikini back at the hotel, the one that collapsed and died, only to get back up and come after you. *Another zombie, then.* Stage two of the howler infection. Walking death. Possessed with a hunger for the flesh of the living.

A second zombie appears, this one a man, clothes also bloody and in disarray. He too approaches the bars, reaches through, stands there staring at you and moaning, always moaning. A third zombie joins the party. Then a fourth. You sit there staring at them, wondering what you should do, how the hell you're going to get out of this. Yeah, you're safe for now but you can't stay in here forever. God only knows when help might arrive.

A sudden noise, terribly loud in the enclosed space. One of the zombie's heads practically explodes and it collapses to the floor. You cover your ears as more gunshots erupt, as more zombies fall down. Soon, all four of them are dead, really dead this time, lying there silent and unmoving.

A police officer steps into view, approaches the cell door, uses a ring of keys to unlock and open it.

"Come on," he tells you. "We need to get out of here."

It's the same cop who arrested you and had you put in this cell in the first place. His rain coat's gone, his uniform spattered with blood. You know you should be angry with him but, right now, you're pretty happy to see him. He removes the clip from his handgun and slaps a new one in. You stand from the bench and move toward the open doorway. Leaving the cell, you have to step over one of the bodies.

"Lets' go," the cop says. He turns and heads in the same direction the other officer fled a short while ago. Around a corner, the hall ends at a doorway with an exit sign over it.

"What's out there?" you ask, stopping in front of the doorway.

"Parking area behind the building," says the cop.

With that, he opens the door.

The rain still falls although maybe not quite as hard as before. A cement walkway leads to a parking lot that can hold maybe two dozen cars. More than half the spots are empty. A tall chain link fence marks the perimeter of the lot. You count seven figures out there milling around between the cars.

More zombies.

95

Floodlights bathe the area in luminescence. As you watch, the figures turn one by one and move toward you. You can hear them moaning over the hiss of the falling rain.

Reaching out, you take hold of the officer's shirtsleeve. "Hold on a second."

He turns and looks at you, his expression grim. "If we're going, we have to go now."

At the sight of those walking, hungry dead folks and the thought of all the other ones that must be out there, you wonder if leaving the somewhat protective confines of the police station is really that great of an idea.

If staying right where you are seems like the more sensible decision, turn to page 105.

If you decide the police officer's plan is undoubtedly the better one, proceed to page 109.

Escape from Zombie Island

—————————————→ ←—————————————

You start to go but then realize someone's still holding your arm. It's Trent, of course. He shakes his head "no" when you look at him. "You'll be much better off staying here. Trust me."

You're not so sure, though. You saw what the woman did. She's the type of person who might actually get you out of this mess.

"I'm going," you tell Trent. "You can come with me if you want."

He lets go of your arm.

You place a hand on his shoulder and say, "Thanks for helping me out when you did. I really appreciate it."

When you head for the doorway he doesn't follow. You give him one last look then head outside and hurry after the woman.

She moves at a brisk pace, almost a run. You hear screaming from across the street, look over to see what has to be a pack of howlers chasing after a fleeing man. Up ahead, several people rush from the neon lit entrance of a nightclub. A young lady turns and points back toward the club and shouts, "There's a bunch of maniacs in there!"

You continue on through the rain toward an intersection where a yellow light blinks overhead. More shouting and screaming erupts from behind you. At the intersection, the woman takes a left and follows the cross street. You pass several small houses with fairly wide yards. After traveling a few blocks, the woman stops at a mailbox marked with the number 314 then follows a cement walkway over to the porch of the humble abode waiting there. After pulling a ring of keys from her pants pocket, she opens the front door of the house and ushers you inside.

The door closes and you hear her fumbling with a light switch on the wall.

"Damn power's out," she says. "Wait here."

You stand there in the dark for maybe a minute before the woman returns holding a flashlight, some candles, and a box of matches. Now you can see you're in a small living room furnished with a couch, a coffee table, and a pair of comfortable looking chairs. The woman leaves again, comes back with some towels and tosses you one. After drying yourself as best you can, you sit on the couch while the woman lights two candles and sets them on the coffee table. Then she pulls a gun from the front of her pants—the same gun she took from the cop back at the station—and sets it on the coffee table next to one of the candles. After this she settles onto one of the chairs and looks at you in the flickering illumination.

"Hell of a night, huh?"

You lean back, try to let some of the tension ease out of your body.

"Yeah, I guess you could say that."

The woman sighs and shakes her head. "I was trying to warn people when that idiot came along and arrested me. I'd seen what some of those freaks, those... I don't know... Whatever you want to call them"

"Howlers," you offer.

She gives a nod. "Howlers. That sounds about right. Anyway... I was only trying to let people know something messed up was going on. And that's when that damned cop got all authoritative on me. Cuffed me. Brought me over to the station. You were there for the rest of it."

"Yeah, that was quite the escape you pulled off."

She laughs a little. "The cop wasn't too bright. When I went for his gun, it took him completely by surprise. Easy enough to coerce him into unlocking the cuffs after that."

"Well, thanks for getting me out of there."

She waves it off like it was nothing. "Natalie Miller, by the way."

You tell her your name.

"Quite the situation we've found ourselves in here," she says.

"We seem safe enough for now."

"Yeah, for now. But if those things keep multiplying..." She purses her lips and shakes her head. "Think about this. If each of them manages to infect only one other person every ten minutes or so, within an hour there would be sixty-four of them. Now imagine ten of them doing that. A hundred. The whole island would be overrun in no time."

You sit there in silence for a few moments, taking in the idea of the entire island falling prey to the howlers.

"I was there when it began," you say after a particularly loud

Escape from Zombie Island

blast of thunder rattles the framed pictures hanging on the walls. You tell her about the airplane crash landing on the beach. The pilot tossing the metal canister free of the burning cockpit. The would-be rescuers breathing in the black gas. All of it.

"USAF," says Natalie. "You're sure?"

"Yeah, I'm sure."

"Unbelievable... So the rumors were true."

In response to your questioning look, she tells you about the eight years she spent in the army, the tours she did in Iraq and Afghanistan.

"People like to talk. Just like anywhere else, I suppose, any other job. Only when you're in the military the rumor mill can be about things like... oh, I don't know... experimental weaponry, maybe. Or chemical warfare. Fun stuff like that. So one night, there's a small group of us hanging out. We've got a little down time and someone's managed to get their hands on a bottle of whiskey. This fellow named Kirkpatrick who's got a little bit of rank on the rest of us, he starts going on about *zombies*, of all things. As in the dead people who get up and walk around, try to eat the living type of zombies. About how he's heard talk that the whole idea might not be so far-fetched after all. That maybe one of the branches of the military—he doesn't know which one; could be more than one, for all he knows—is working on a type of chemical weapon that could turn everyday, normal people into ravenous, flesh-eating corpses. 'Can you imagine?' he asks with this big grin on his face. 'You get a plane behind enemy lines and drop a bunch of this stuff on a heavily populated area. Widespread panic. Total chaos. Not to mention the number of casualties...'"

Natalie gives a little snort of laughter and shakes her head. "We all thought Kirkpatrick was full of you know what, of course. Talking out his rather sizable behind." She motions toward the front door. "But after seeing what's going on out there... Maybe he wasn't so full of you know what after all."

Natalie gets to her feet, asks if you're hungry. When you say you could eat she heads toward the kitchen, tells you she's got a portable propane stove "in case of an emergency." Twenty minutes later you're sitting at the kitchen table, a burning candle standing at its center, eating a bowl of chicken soup and a couple slices of bread. When your bowl is empty and the bread is gone, Natalie gets up and goes to the fridge, pulls out two bottled beers, opens them and sets one in front of you. Then she sits back down, looks across the table at you.

"We'll have to make a break for it."

You've been wondering when she would get around to this particular subject. After all, it's not like the two of you can just sit around here, chatting and drinking beer and hoping that the little epidemic breaking loose across the island will magically go away.

"I needed a little time to think about our situation, didn't want to rush into anything," says Natalie as if reading your mind. "If there's one thing I learned in the military it's that planning is the key to success. That and discipline." She smiles. "I guess there were two things I learned." After a long swig of beer, she sets the bottle down and sighs appreciatively. "We need to get off this island while we still can." She pushes her chair back from the table and stands up. "Go ahead and finish your beer. In five minutes we're moving out."

With that she turns and walks out of the room.

Proceed to page 121.

Escape from Zombie Island

Sure, you want to live through this, but you don't think this woman will help you achieve that goal. In fact, if you go with her it might be her reckless behavior that gets you killed. So you stand there and watch as she pushes her way through the doors at the building's entrance and disappears into the night.

"Good call," says Trent as he lets go of your arm. "She's nothing but trouble. And there's plenty of that going around already."

You look at the bodies of the howlers lying on the floor, all too aware of the fact more of them can arrive at any moment.

"Okay, so what now?" you wonder aloud.

"Now we make our own exit," says Trent. "Come on."

He moves toward the entranceway.

"Hey you, come back here," says the police officer from behind the counter, now getting to his feet. "You're witnesses to a crime. You can't leave."

"Watch us," you tell him.

Outside, you hurry through the rain over to the car. Luckily no howlers get in your way. You open the passenger side door, hop in and buckle up as Trent starts the car and pulls away from the curb.

"Where are we going?" you ask.

"Not sure yet," he says. "Anywhere but here."

As far as plans go, it's not a very good one. But for right now it's all that either of you have so you're going to have to live with it. During the brief time spent inside the police station the situation around here has noticeably worsened. People run to and fro across the street. You hear the unmistakable sound of gunshots from somewhere nearby and the *boom* of an explosion from further down the street. Yeah, "anywhere but here" might not be a great plan but it sure beats sticking around these parts any longer than necessary.

Trent makes it to the intersection a block from the station where he hangs a right, gives the car some gas and takes off down the open road in front of you. Sitting there quietly, you try to figure out where the two of you should go. Maybe if you can reach the airport... It seems like it would offer the best opportunity for getting off the island.

"Damn, look at that," says Trent, distracting you from your

101

thoughts.

He slows the car and pulls over to the right hand side of the road. Through the window you see what got his attention: A man limps along the sidewalk, head bowed, obviously injured. Judging by the amount of blood on his shirt you'd guess he's been hurt pretty badly. Even still, you don't want Trent to stop, not for anything. But then you think about where you'd be if he hadn't stopped when you needed help. *Probably in a pretty bad spot.* So you can't begrudge him for pulling over now. You guess it's just the type of guy he is.

The car nears the curb, slowing down to match the injured man's pace. Your window lowers automatically and Trent leans toward you, speaks loud enough to be heard over the rain: "Hey, buddy! How badly are you hurt?"

At first the guy doesn't respond, doesn't react in any way. Head lowered, he keeps limping along.

Maybe's he's in shock.

You can only guess at what he went through to sustain those injuries.

"Do you need a doctor?" asks Trent.

The guy finally stops. He stands there like he's deep in thought, maybe even pondering the mysteries of the universe. All the while, you become increasingly convinced there's something not quite right with this picture. Not that you think the guy's a howler. If so, more than likely he would have attacked the vehicle by now. No, something else then. Exactly what it is, though, you can't say for sure.

The injured man turns and looks at you, starts to move toward the vehicle.

"Uh, Trent."

Those eyes… Gray and glassy. An emptiness there. They make you think of death.

A walking dead man.

Just outside the vehicle now, you can hear him groaning as he leans down toward the open window.

"Trent, I really think we should—"

The man lunges at you, face first, buries his teeth into the side of your neck, pulls free a sizeable chunk of skin and muscle and torn strands of artery. Trent curses and hits the gas, tearing away from the

Escape from Zombie Island

curb and the man who attacked you. Reaching up, you use your hands to staunch the blood literally pouring from the gaping hole in your neck. Trent says something about a hospital and that he's sorry, so damned sorry...

The light from the dashboard and passing streetlamps grows dim. Trent's voice, the revving of the car's engine and the tapping of the rain on the roof become less distinct. You imagine these sounds reaching you from the end of a long tunnel, one that keeps getting longer and longer as you sit there feeling the blood, all that blood slipping through your fingers. A deep and pervasive coldness settles into your bones. The night rushes in from outside the car and floods the whole of your being. And then you feel nothing, not even a sense of regret that some slow, stupid zombie was able to take you out like that.

THE END

Ray Wallace

Escape from Zombie Island

———————————————→ ←———————————————

You shake your head.

"There's no way I'm going out there."

The cop shrugs. "Suit yourself." Then, without another word, he steps through the doorway and runs off into the night.

You pull the door closed, blocking the sight of the fleeing cop and the walking dead people. Standing there, you think back to the four zombies the cop put down outside the holding cell and wonder how many more might be inside the building. You need to find somewhere safe to hole up for a while, somewhere the zombies won't be able to get you. Now that you think about it, you wish the officer had never come along and freed you from the cell. *I was safe in there*. Maybe there's a way to lock the door without a key. If not, you'll have to find somewhere else to hide. *A storage space or an attic, maybe?*

You walk back and peek around the corner, gaze along the main length of the hallway, take in the sight of the bodies lying on the floor. A closed doorway stands at the far end of the corridor. Past the holding cell along the right hand wall, you know another doorway leads into the room with the desks where you were booked and had your mugshot taken. Gathering your courage, you make your way down the hallway as quietly as you can, stepping carefully past the corpses at your feet. Then you stop and peer into the room with the desks. And what you see in there makes you wish all the more you'd never left the holding cell in the first place.

Zombies. A good half dozen of them. All kneeling down in a rough circle on the floor, a pair of legs wearing the dark blue pants of a police uniform sticking out from between two of the undead creatures. The sound of their feeding causes your flesh to crawl. As you watch, one of the zombies reaches up into the air, a long, ropy strand of what can only be intestine in its hand. Then it leans its head back and lowers the awful treat toward its mouth.

You need to get out of here, a tiny voice in the back of your mind keeps saying, growing louder with each passing second. *Now*. You try not to panic, don't want to do anything rash but it's kind of tough when faced with the terrible scene laid out before you.

And then you see the gun. It's right there, on the floor, maybe

105

ten feet away, about half the distance between you and the pack of feasting zombies. Before you can change your mind, you step into the room and walk toward the gun, bring your feet down as softly as you can on the linoleum tiling, not wanting to make a sound. The zombies moan and groan, grunt and growl and go on chewing, oblivious to your presence for the time being.

This is actually going to work.

You stand next to the gun, heart racing as every survival instinct in your body tells you to flee this place. Fighting the nearly overwhelming urge to turn and run, you crouch down and grab the weapon.

A scream tears its way through the room.

Actually, it's more like a *howl*.

You turn and look past the rows of desks, over toward the other doorway, the one leading out to the lobby of the police station. A woman strides through that doorway, long hair wet and straggly around her face. Wide, manic eyes. When she sees you she lets loose with another one of those awful howling shrieks.

The zombies pause in their feast. Three of them stand and give you their full attention, eyes dull, mouths coated with blood as they continue chewing and moaning, always with the moaning. The weapon in your hand makes you feel a little better about your predicament. Not that you're any sort of trained marksperson. The truth is, you've never fired a gun before in your life.

How hard can it be?

You've seen it done countless times on TV and in the movies. Just point it and pull the trigger. *Blam!* Easy as that.

You back away as the walking corpses shamble in your direction. Right now, though, they're not the real threat. The howler screams again and rushes past the desks, pushes her way through the small crowd of zombies in her haste to reach you, seemingly unaware or uncaring of the gun in your hand.

Put her down!

You stop in the doorway. The howler's so close you couldn't *not* hit her, even with your lack of experience. You aim the gun and squeeze the trigger.

It doesn't fire.

The howler closes in.

Escape from Zombie Island

No, no, no...

You look at the gun in disbelief, like it's decided to pull the world's biggest practical joke on you, one that you find anything but funny. Then you notice the small lever on the side of the gun above the grip. How many shows have you seen where someone's been told to check the safety? You push the lever up with your thumb. By now the howler is practically on top of you, mouth open wide, ready to grab you and breathe the black gas into your face. When her hand settles onto your shoulder you press the gun against her stomach and pull the trigger again.

This time it fires.

The howler stops dead in her tracks.

Two more shots: *Blam! Blam!* Then there's nothing but a clicking sound as you pull the trigger a few more times, the clip now empty. Those three shots, though, they did the trick. The howler collapses, doesn't look like she's going anywhere anytime soon. The zombies, however, continue to move closer. Dropping the now useless gun to the floor, you turn and run down the hallway, past the holding cell once again, around the corner and over to the door where you stood with the police officer only a short while ago. Looks like you have to leave the station after all. And now you have to do it alone.

Pushing the door open, you take in the sight of the parking lot, the figures out there still wandering around in the rain.

As long as I keep moving they won't be able to catch me.

Over to your right, you see a rolling gate where cars would enter and leave the lot. It stands open. More than a few zombies have gathered there. Still, you're pretty sure you can evade them if you decide to go out that way. To your left you see fewer of the walking dead folk. You might be better off heading over there and scaling the fence instead.

If you think you should leave through the gate, turn to page 125.

If you want to try the fence instead, proceed to page 131.

Ray Wallace

Escape from Zombie Island

$\longrightarrow \quad \longleftarrow$

You follow the cop through the doorway. A fence encloses the parking lot. Over to the right a rolling gate stands open. It doesn't take a rocket scientist to realize this is where the dead folk have been entering the lot. Several of them wander around near the gate. Without hesitation, the cop heads directly toward them. You hope he knows what he's doing considering you're counting on him to get you out of here alive. As he approaches the gate he lifts his handgun and opens fire.

Zombies stagger back from the attack. The ones taking shots to the head drop to the ground and stop moving. The two of you pass through the gate and circle around to the front of the building. The cruiser sits in the same spot where it was left when you arrived at the station.

"It's unlocked," says the cop as he approaches the car and circles around to the driver's side.

You open the passenger side door and get in. Never in your life could you imagine such a feeling of relief at being inside a police car. The officer starts the car and drives off.

"Now what?" you ask him.

He shakes his head. "I have no idea."

Well, that doesn't reassure you very much.

The cop flicks a switch activating the lights on top of the vehicle.

"I guess we should head for the coastline." He shrugs. "Less people there. Less of those… things."

The officer executes a three point turn and heads back in the opposite direction from which you first arrived.

The general state of affairs around here has dramatically worsened while you were locked up in your cozy little cell. Obviously, the howlers have been spreading their military grade infection. What had been a stretch of road dedicated to fun and revelry with its restaurants and night clubs has been transformed into something out of a nightmare. Ahead, flames leap from the front of a building. A burning car sits in the middle of the road and you can see another one a block further along. People run into the street and along the sidewalks while packs of slower moving figures go

109

stumbling by. In the circle of light cast by a nearby streetlamp, you see a man surrounded, bitten and clawed at by a trio of zombies.

The cop keeps the car going at a leisurely pace, slowing even further when someone crosses in front of it or a zombie passes by. At one point a guy wearing a baseball cap walks backward into the street, completely oblivious to any approaching traffic as he fires a handgun toward the sidewalk. When he turns and looks directly into the approaching headlights of the police cruiser, you can see the terror etched onto his face. He comes over and pounds on your window then curses and runs off when he realizes the car isn't going to stop.

At an intersection the cop slams on the brakes as a pickup truck, following the cross street, flies through, nearly plowing into the front of the car.

"Damned idiot!" says the cop. He turns onto the cross street and you wonder if he's going after the truck, if he plans to pull it over and write the driver a ticket. But instead he says, "We've got to get off this road. There's just way to much action around these parts."

A block down and already things look a lot calmer over here. Less foot traffic means fewer monsters chasing people around. The cop hits the gas, eases the car up to around thirty miles an hour. Then, without warning, a woman dashes from the sidewalk and into the street, waving her hands at the cruiser, trying to get it to stop. You put your hands out in front of you, brace them against the dash as the cop stomps the brakes and turns the wheel to keep from running the woman down. The cruiser misses the woman but ends up crashing into the back of a parked car with enough force to deploy the airbags.

While issuing a string of curse words, the cop releases the catch on his seatbelt, pushes open the driver's side door and immediately discovers the reason behind the woman's reckless behavior. Hands grab him and pull him free of the vehicle. He shouts something incomprehensible, the sound mixing with the awful moaning of the zombies outside. You see more of the undead creatures moving toward you through the passenger side window. After opening the door on your side of the car, you waste precious time fighting with the airbag. By the time you exit the vehicle several zombies wait to greet you.

Escape from Zombie Island

What happens next isn't pretty. To put it bluntly, it's a bad way to go.

THE END

Ray Wallace

Escape from Zombie Island

During your time in the hospital, the intensity of the rain seems to have lessened a bit. Instead of a downpour, you make your way through something more like a steady drizzle. You can only hope this means the storm will soon depart. Now, if you can only find a way to do the same thing and leave the island behind altogether.

As you reach the end of the hospital building, you see a parking lot half filled with cars. Streetlamps illuminate the area. A couple of figures stagger around between the cars over there.

Probably shouldn't get too close.

You continue along the sidewalk toward an intersection with a blinking red light. You really have no idea where you're going, which way north or south or any other direction lies. Are you heading back toward the hotel? Away from it? Toward the airport where you landed upon your arrival?

The airport.

Of course. Where better to find a way off this damned island? The odds of meeting someone with a boat capable of taking you back to the mainland seem rather long. No, you have to get to the northern tip of the island where the airport is located which means you have to find a ride.

A car approaches and you wave your hands for it to stop. It keeps going though, makes a left at the intersection, fishtailing across the wet pavement as it speeds off and out of sight. You curse under your breath but can't really blame the driver. With all that's been going on around here this evening, you wonder if you would have acted any differently.

Looking back along the sidewalk, you see you're being followed. Your pursuers don't appear to be in any sort of hurry, more like a couple of drunks staggering along at the end of a particularly rough bender. Nonetheless, you decide to pick up the pace a bit, break into a leisurely jog as you reach the intersection and make your way across to the other side.

Three blocks later, you're already a bit winded—funny how much undergoing an operation will take out of you—and slow your progress to a more leisurely pace. Another car whizzes by without stopping even though you shout and wave your hands. You need to

113

think of a way to get a ride here real soon. Walking across the island appeals to you less with every block you cover.

A few minutes later, you hear shouting followed by the unmistakable sound of gunfire—*pop! pop! pop!*—from somewhere dead ahead. You stop, deciding it might be a good time to double back to the last intersection and find a different route out of here. And you're about to do exactly that when a scream, an inhuman *howl* emerges from the darkness behind you. Looking back, you see a man in a pair of shorts and a tattered shirt sprinting directly toward you.

So much for that idea.

You take off running, wondering how much energy you've got left, how long you can keep this up.

Not long.

Ahead, you see another intersection, another blinking light. Once there, you turn left around the building at the corner, hoping a hiding place presents itself, somewhere you can rest and, with any luck, lose the howler.

The fronts of bars, nightclubs and restaurants line this new road, neon lights adding to the illumination cast by the streetlamps overhead. A burning car catches your attention as do the flames licking the face of a nightclub a few buildings down. You hear more gunfire and shouting, both louder now. A group of six or seven well dressed people—the men wear slacks and long sleeved shirts, the women tight skirts and high heels—emerge in a rush from the front of a bar maybe twenty feet in front of you. One of the women trips and falls to the pavement, yelling at the others to wait, "Please wait!" Her cries fall on deaf ears. Before she can regain her footing two lurching figures step out of the bar and grab her. You avert your gaze and hurry past the scene not wanting to see what comes next. Besides, you have more pressing concerns, like the howler who's still chasing after you, not to mention your rapidly fading endurance. And let's not forget about the pulsing agony in your shoulder where you had a bullet removed only a few hours ago. Sucking in air, you push yourself to go faster, *faster*, even as you inevitably slow down.

The howler tackles you from behind and the two of you crash to the pavement. The pain in your shoulder explodes and the world around you goes black.

Escape from Zombie Island

Lights out...

You come to with the howler on top of you, pinning you down. Weak and winded, you lie there on your back as he leans in like he's going to give you a big, sloppy, open mouthed kiss. As bad as this might be, what he actually does is much worse. He *exhales*... A black cloud flows out of his mouth. You try to resist but in the end find you have no choice but to pull the howler's infectious breath deep into your lungs.

As you start to choke the howler stands up, gazes down at you for a little while before departing. A feeling of pure electricity crackles along the lengths of your nervous system. You thrash about where you lie on the concrete. The whole of your being has become nothing more than a crushing, searing mass of pain. All thoughts of who you are, of *what* you are, all memories of the life you have led, of the people you have known and loved vanish from your mind. An eternity passes before the agony mercifully, blissfully diminishes. By the time it disappears completely an overriding compulsion consumes you:

Find other hosts. Exhale the black gas. Spread the infection.

When the last of the convulsions ease from your body you roll over, push up onto your hands and knees then rise to your feet.

"Uh, uh. Sorry, but you're one of them now."

That voice is the last thing you ever hear. It belongs to a man with a beard, a baseball cap, and a big shiny pistol who puts you down. Just like that, your time as a howler ends before it ever begins. And to think of all the fun you could have had...

THE END

Ray Wallace

Escape from Zombie Island

→ ←

Left it is. Call it a hunch. Hopefully one that will pay off.

The rain continues to fall and you think about how much you'd rather be inside somewhere nice and dry. But for now you have to keep moving. It's not safe around these parts, obviously. Wherever "these parts" are exactly.

As you walk along the sidewalk a pair of cars races by. You wave at them, try to get them to stop but to no avail. Soon enough they disappear from view. The sky flickers with lightning; the resulting thunder sounds more like a grumble than a roar. After a minute or so of walking, another vehicle approaches. *Police cruiser*, you assume upon seeing the row of lights, currently dormant, mounted to the roof. And even though it was a police officer who shot you, and who you hold largely responsible for your current predicament, you feel a surge of hope and excitement. A little help from law enforcement would really come in handy right about now. No point in holding a grudge when your very survival is at stake. Once again, though, you can't get the car to stop. You see the word "security" on its door as it goes by and realize it's not a police cruiser anyway. Even still, a ride's a ride. Getting rescued by a cop would have been an added bonus.

You approach an intersection with a four way stop. A church stands on the corner, steeple jutting toward the sky. Beyond the church you see a group of figures crossing to your side of the street. The way some of them limp along—one of them appears to be missing an arm—gives you a bad feeling. Looks like more of the same type of creature you had to deal with back at the hospital. As you watch, another half a dozen of them head into the street, visible in the light cast by the streetlamp near the sidewalk. You stop, deciding it might be a good time to turn around, head back the other way, hope the going is easier in that direction.

A terrible howling sound cuts through the silence behind you. Glancing over your shoulder, you see two people running your way. They can't be more than a hundred feet behind you.

The zombies will be easier to elude.

Or so you hope.

You run straight ahead, directly toward the group of walking dead people. And it turns out you assumed correctly. Even fatigued and weakened, you find there's enough room to evade them easily enough. In the end, all they can do is moan and watch you go by.

The howlers continue their pursuit. Not that you expected them to give up. Less than a minute into the chase and already you find it more difficult to breathe. Damn, that surgery really did take a lot out of you. A look back shows you the distance between you and your pursuers has noticeably diminished. You run for all your worth, hoping for a miracle because without one the howlers are sure to catch you soon enough. And after that…

Gunfire erupts from behind you. Another backward glance and you see a black van pulling up next to the group of zombies. More gunfire and zombies fall to the pavement. Then one of the howler's goes down. Its partner, however, keeps coming after you with everything he's got. Tiny black dots dance before your eyes. Gasping for air, you slow down. Whatever reserves of endurance have brought you this far have reached their limit. Knowing you can't outrun the inevitable, you stop and turn, hands on your knees, wanting to face what's about to happen rather than let it sneak up on you.

The van sits idling near the fallen zombies. "Go, go, go!" you hear someone shout. The driver gives it some gas causing the tires to spin out on the wet road. The howler, a young man with a buzz cut, keeps running, can't be more than twenty feet from you now. Fifteen… Ten… Five… Finally, knowing he has you, he slows to a walk, tilts his head to the side and screams. Behind him, halfway down the block, the van picks up speed. A figure in black hangs out the side door of the vehicle, aiming a handgun in your general direction. It's a bad angle, though. The shooter has about as much of a chance of hitting you as the howler. And you've been shot enough for one evening, thank you very much. Although, considering the alternative, taking another bullet may not be the worst thing to happen to you tonight.

The howler stops less than an arm's length in front of you, reaches out to you like an old friend looking for a hug. He places a hand on your shoulder, opens his mouth, no doubt ready to exhale the black gas he carries inside of him. Reflexively, you step back as he lunges toward you.

Escape from Zombie Island

So this is it, you have time to think. *End of the line...*

Then, quite unexpectedly, the howler's expression transforms into one of almost comic surprise. He lowers his hand, staggers to the side and drops to the ground where he shakes his head back and forth, kicking his legs a bit. You've seen this before with the bikini clad girl in the hotel's stairwell.

Zombie time.

And just when you needed a miracle.

The van pulls up and stops next to you and the fallen howler. The figure in black turns out to be a middle-aged man with a well groomed, mostly gray beard. He gets out through the open side door, looks down at the thrashing howler then aims his gun and pulls the trigger. The howler stops moving as the gunshot echoes into the distance.

"Sorry we couldn't get here sooner," he tells you.

"I'm glad you're here now," you manage to respond.

"Get in," he says and motions toward the van. "Grab a seat in back. You look like you need to get off your feet for a little while."

When you don't move he steps over to you, lets you place an arm around his shoulders and leads you toward the waiting vehicle.

"We're gonna try to find a way off this God forsaken island," the man tells you as you climb into the van. "You're welcome to tag along if you want."

Sounds good to you. Looks like your luck might be changing. Who knows? Maybe you'll find a way to survive this night after all.

Turn to page 133.

Ray Wallace

Escape from Zombie Island

————————————→ ←————————————

When Natalie returns she carries a pair of handguns with her, holds one out to you. Feeling a touch of anxiety, you take it.

"You ever fire one of these before?" she asks.

You tell her you haven't.

"Simplest thing in the world. Make sure the safety's off. That little lever there. Then point it and pull the trigger. " She shrugs. "Pretty much all there is to it."

"If you say so."

"And don't worry." She smiles. "It's not the cop's gun, in case you're wondering."

Actually, you weren't. But now that she's brought it up...

"Don't you think the police will want it back, maybe come looking for it?"

"I think they have more important things to worry about." She gestures toward the gun in your hand. "By the way, it's loaded. And with any luck it will stay that way. Gotta prepare for the worst though. And with the way things are going out there, I think we have to expect it."

A minute later finds you in the cramped one car garage next to Natalie's house, staring at the vehicle parked there: a jeep with a soft top, big knobby tires, and roll bars. Except for the red paint job, it looks like the sort of vehicle Natalie may have driven while in the military. You open the passenger side door and climb in, set the handgun on your lap with your hand on top of it. Natalie hops in behind the wheel, uses the remote she's got clipped to the visor to open the garage door. Then she starts the jeep, puts it in gear and drives out into the storm.

At the end of the driveway she takes a left and heads back toward the town's main strip, the long section of road where the bars, the nightclubs, and the police station are located. You think about Trent, wonder where he's at, how he's doing right now. Mrs. Rinehart, too. Trent made his choice to stay behind so even though you wish him the best you don't feel too bad about deserting him. Mrs. Rinehart, on the other hand... You really wanted to help her, hated having to abandon her like that.

What's done is done.

121

The only thing you can do now is keep moving forward and hope to find a way out of this mess.

You look over at Natalie in the soft glow of the dashboard lights. She wears her shoulder length hair in a ponytail and a grim expression on her face letting you know she's all business.

"So what's the plan?" you ask.

"First we take a look and assess the situation locally. If it has deteriorated we leave town. Head north." You like her assertiveness, her confidence. Good to know you're riding with someone who seems to know what she's doing.

"North? Why north?" you ask.

"The airport. I think if we're going to find a way off this island it will be there."

As soon as Natalie turns back onto nightclub row, as you've come to think of it, you can tell the situation has, in fact, deteriorated.

The streetlamps glare down on a scene straight out of a disaster movie. People scurry along the sidewalks and into the street. A car burns in the middle of the road. Thick clouds of smoke billow out of a building a short distance ahead.

Natalie stops the jeep to keep from running anybody over. As you sit there, a man steps into the beams of the jeep's headlights. Through the rain you can see the fear and confusion on his face as three lurching figures slowly but inexorably close in on him. He turns in a circle, unsure of which way to run. His hesitation proves to be his undoing. One of the figures, a woman limping badly on a foot turned at a painful looking angle, comes up behind the man and wraps her arms around him. The two other figures converge, lean in and tear into the man's neck and shoulders with their teeth. The woman holding him from behind uses her mouth to snap at his ear like a vicious dog. Then the group loses its collective balance and topples over, falling hard to the pavement.

"Yeah, they look like zombies all right," says Natalie in a decidedly nonchalant tone of voice. You look over at her, amazed she can remain so calm in the face of such brutality. "I guess we need to find another way out of here."

She puts the jeep in reverse and gives it some gas. You hear the *thud* of an impact. The vehicle rises and falls as if going over a speed

Escape from Zombie Island

bump then continues to back up. You see the man who's been run over lying in the road, reaching out with one hand toward the jeep, fingers grasping, mouth opening and closing.

"Got one," says Natalie with a laugh. "Fifty points."

She backs all the way to the intersection then puts the jeep in first gear, turns left and hits the accelerator. As she drives you sit there quietly, wrap your fingers around the grip of the handgun, think about the woman who gave it you. She might be a little on the crazy side but maybe crazy's what you need right about now.

Several minutes pass and Natalie guides the jeep onto a four lane highway you find vaguely familiar. It looks like the same stretch of road the shuttle took from the airport upon your arrival, although now you're going in the opposite direction. The jeep cruises along at forty-five miles per hour, the rain battering the thick cloth above your head like a swarm of mutant, blood sucking insects trying to get in. Cars drive by the other way and you can't help but wonder if the people inside those vehicles have any idea what awaits them. Although it's entirely possible things aren't any better where you're headed. Who knows how far the howlers have spread the infection by now?

The jeep ascends a long rise in the road. As you head down the other side Natalie tenses and shouts, "Hold on!" then stomps the brake pedal. The jeep goes into a long skid, spinning slowly. For a moment, it feels like it might tip over. *Guess that's what the roll bars are for*. By the time the vehicle stops you can see the massive tree lying across the road, blocking traffic moving in either direction.

"Damn it!" says Natalie as she thumps her fist on the steering wheel. She backs the jeep over to the side of the road and puts it in park. Another car approaches, slows down and stops well short of the fallen tree before making a u-turn and heading back the other way.

"Is there another route to the airport?" you ask, heart racing from the near collision with the tree.

Natalie shrugs. "Not that I'm aware of."

She opens the driver's side door and hops out into the storm, closing the door behind her. You watch as she walks over to the tree and maneuvers herself in between a couple of thick branches, disappearing from view. While she's gone two more cars arrive before turning around and leaving. Eventually, Natalie reappears and heads back to the jeep, opens the door and gets in, thoroughly drenched. She looks at you and says, "Well, I guess that settles it. We proceed on foot from here."

"That settles it?"

A shrug. "Unless you want to turn around and go back. You can take the jeep. All I ask is that you leave it in front of my house. I'm not going back, though. One way or another, I'm getting to that airport and then getting the hell off this island."

As she finishes speaking, a bolt of lightning snakes down out of the sky, so close the world outside turns bright for half a second. The resulting *boom* causes the floor to vibrate beneath your feet. Braving a storm like this on foot sounds like a really bad idea. You still have to be a couple of miles from the airport. And who knows how many howlers and zombies might be waiting between here and there.

If there's no way you're getting out and walking the rest of the way to the airport, turn to page 137.

If you decide to stick with Natalie since she's gotten you this far, proceed to page 141.

Escape from Zombie Island

You head for the gate, knowing it offers the easiest way out of the parking lot. As if on cue, the zombies gathered there turn in your direction, some of them reaching toward you, moaning all the while. You approach the gate at a jog, hoping that if you move quickly enough none of the zombies will be able to grab hold of you. The strategy pays off and you make your way past them with relative ease, experience only one close call when you have to push a teenage boy wearing a Rammstein t-shirt out of your way. After that, you encounter no other problems as you circle around to the front of the police station.

Once there, you stop and look toward the street in front of the building, see only a few zombies wandering about. You hear screaming in the distance, the kind that lets you know there's at least one howler in the vicinity. You seem safe enough for the time being though.

To get out of town and off this island you need a vehicle of some sort. You know you'll have to make your way to the coast or, better yet, the airport at the north tip of the island. The odds of reaching either destination on foot do not seem particularly favorable. So you can either hitch a ride or try to steal one of your own. You think about the gun you left behind in the police station. It could have proved useful, even with an empty clip, in the event you do decide to take someone's car. No point in worrying about it now because there is no way you're going back to get it.

You head toward the street, stop at the sidewalk and take a look in both directions, try to assess the situation. To your right, about a block away, a number of zombies wander around. Several more of them kneel in a tight circle in the middle of the road. Remembering what you saw inside the police station, you can make a fairly educated guess as to what they might be doing. Off to your left you see what can only be described as total chaos. A car burns in the middle of the road, blocking traffic. Further down, flames leap outward from the windows of a building. People frantically run about, chased by other figures, plainly visible in the light cast by the streetlamps lining the road. You hear screaming, random gunfire, blaring alarms. And then, from behind you, a very particular type of screaming.

Howling.

You know you can't stay here. You have to move. Now.

To your right things appear somewhat calmer, maybe a bit safer. So you turn that way, ready to do some more zombie dodging—you pulled it off once, no reason you can't do it again—when a cop emerges from the front entrance of the police department and shouts, "Die you flesh eating sons of bitches!" He points a really big gun toward the street and pulls the trigger, firing round after round at the zombies there, shouting all the while, his words drowned out by the explosive sounds generated by the weapon in his hand.

Where did he come from?

You don't recall seeing him during your time inside the station. Not that it really matters. What *does* matter is staying out of the line of fire. And so you change directions, go left instead, over toward the burning car and the chaos beyond.

Soon you're in the thick of it. Zombies, zombies everywhere... They wander around in packs, surround people, close in on them, attack and feed upon them. Howlers run by, shrieking in that awful way they like to do. As you watch, one of them tackles a woman right in front of you, pins her down and breathes the black gas into her face. The smell of smoke lies thick upon the air. Gunfire adds an offbeat, staccato rhythm to the sights and sounds of violence and mayhem calling for your attention from all sides.

Dead ahead you see the source of much of the gunfire you've been hearing. Three men in black suits stand in front of the entrance to one of the buildings, firing handguns toward the street. As you approach them you wave your arms and shout, "Don't shoot! I'm not one of them! I'm alive! Don't shoot!!"

The three men—bouncers, judging from the fact they're all about six-five and well over two hundred and fifty pounds—stand behind a red velvet rope. The one nearest you—shaved head, pair of dark glasses—looks toward you, stops firing his weapon, waves you closer. He motions toward the glass doorway behind him plastered with flyers and posters for various DJ's.

"Get inside," he tells you.

"Is it safe in there?" you ask.

A shrug of his massive shoulders. "Safer than out here." He

Escape from Zombie Island

returns his attention to the street and pops off a few more shots.

You open the door and enter the nightclub. A second set of doors stands at the end of a dimly lit corridor before you. Set into the wall of the corridor is an alcove where patrons would normally stop and pay the admission fee. Right now it's deserted so you continue forward then push your way through the second doorway and into a chaos of an altogether different variety.

Lights cut through the darkness like the onset of an alien invasion. The song pouring out of the massive sound system fills the room with its stabbing synths and steady, pounding kick drum. A young woman serves drinks from behind a long bar off to your right. Directly in front of you, the dance floor occupies a large area of the room where twenty or so people move their bodies in time to the music. At the back of the room you see the DJ—florescent green baseball cap turned sideways on his head—up in the booth located a good ten feet above the dance floor.

Looks like these people didn't get the memo about the zombie outbreak currently underway. Or if they did they don't care. Most of them are probably out of their minds on Ecstasy or whatever drugs the club kids are into these days. As long as the power stays on it looks like this party has no intention of shutting down anytime soon.

Since you doubt you'll find anyone on the dance floor willing or able to help you out with a ride, you head over to the bar and wait for a guy with no shirt on to pay for his drink. When he departs you place your hands on the bar and lean toward the young woman standing across from you.

"What can I get for you?" she asks. "Beer? Mixed drink?"

"How about a ride out of here?" you say, trying to raise your voice over the music. When she shakes her head and points to her ear, you repeat the question only louder this time.

"Too drunk to drive?" she shouts back at you. "Want me to call a cab?"

Actually, a cab would be great but you don't think it's a realistic option.

"No, I..." You lean closer, motion for her to do the same. "Are you aware of what's going on outside?"

She nods her head. "Yeah, the weather sucks. Power's gone off a few times. That's why the place is so dead tonight."

She thinks it's dead in here...

127

Before you can reply, a sudden commotion catches your attention, forces you to turn around and see what's going on. A trio of new arrivals—

How did they get in? Did something scare off the bouncers?

—stride into the room with a definite purpose. They lean their heads back and howl loudly enough to compete with the music. Then they rush the dance floor and set about attacking random partiers, all the while exhaling clouds of a black, smoke-like substance from their mouths. A number of people who were dancing and partying like it's 1999 drop to the floor, arms and legs flailing. Then the music stops.

"Hey, what's going on down there?" asks the DJ over the club's PA system. "Everyone needs to chill out and have a good time. We're all about PLUR around here. Drop the bass, not bombs. You know what I'm saying?"

Actually, you don't know what he's saying. *They're all about ploor around here? What is this guy talking about?* The one thing you do know is that you need to get out of here.

You turn back to the bartender, see her standing there, eyes wide with disbelief.

"Do you have a car?" you ask her. She doesn't respond, just stares at the scene taking place behind you. Raising your hand to her face you snap your fingers. "We have to get out of here and we're gonna need a car if we plan on getting off this island alive."

She blinks and focuses her gaze on you. "Yeah, I've got a car. It's parked behind the club." She nods her head toward the DJ booth. "There's an exit over there. We can go out that way."

"Okay, then. Let's do it."

She heads toward the end of the bar and you meet her there. For the first time you get a good look at her outfit. She's dressed all in black: boots, shorts, and a t-shirt tied at the midriff. Dark purple lipstick and piercings through the lip, nose, and eyebrow complete the Goth girl ensemble.

"Come on," you say and lead the way toward the dance floor, step carefully between the people lying there convulsing. The howlers pay them no attention. Their only concern seems to be infecting those still on their feet.

"Over there," says the bartender, pointing toward the entrance to

Escape from Zombie Island

a hallway next to the DJ booth.

As you reach the far side of the dance floor, you start to believe you might walk out of here without incident. But then the bartender stumbles and cries out. One of the howlers has her by the arm, pulling her toward him. She tries to resist but he's got both hands wrapped around her wrist. He opens his mouth wide and leans in toward her. It doesn't take a genius to figure out what's about to happen next...

If you write the bartender off as a lost cause and continue onward alone, proceed to page 145.

If you stop and help her because not only do you need a ride but it's the right thing to do, turn to page 149.

Escape from Zombie Island

→ ←

You jog toward the fence, avoiding the zombies easily enough. The fence rattles when you grab it and start to climb. When you reach the top, you swing one leg and then the other up and over before working your way down the other side. Due to the rain, the metal feels a bit slippery in your hands, enough so that you lose your grip and drop several feet to the ground. You land awkwardly and roll your left ankle, gasp at the sudden flare of pain. Staying on your feet, you curse under your breath as you turn and hobble away, leaving the parking lot and the police station behind.

You're in an alleyway formed by the backs of low buildings. Lights mounted near exit doors illuminate the way forward. Good thing the power's still on as you don't relish the idea of making your way through this place in total darkness. Fifty feet or so in front of you, a car cruises by the mouth of the alleyway. Even slowed by your bad ankle, it shouldn't take you long to get there.

Encouraged by the idea, you pick up the pace despite the pain. With a backward glance you see slow moving figures entering the alleyway behind you. Zombies. They're far enough back that, for the moment, they pose no real threat. But if any howlers decide to show up...

The end of the alleyway can't be more than twenty feet from you now. Where you'll go from there you're not sure. Obviously, you'll have to find someone who can give you a ride, that or obtain a car of your own—in other words, steal one—if you want to have any shot at getting off this island.

Nearing the end of the alleyway, you watch as three figures step into view around the corner of the building just ahead and to your left. These new arrivals stop and look at you for a few seconds. Then one of them, a young woman wearing a tank top and a knee-length skirt, starts in with that awful howling you've come to know too well. You move back as the other two join in. When the screaming falls silent you hear only the rain and the moaning of the zombies reverberating through the alley behind you.

The howlers charge.

You do an about face and run as fast as you can on your bad ankle. More zombies have appeared on the scene since you last looked—a rather large group of them crowds the alleyway in front of you. A desperate situation, to be sure. The way you see it, you can keep moving forward and try to maneuver your way through the throng of walking corpses. (Who knows? You might make it out the other side. *Stranger things have happened*, you suppose.) Or you can stop and turn back around, try to catch the howlers off guard and slip past them. (Again, not the greatest of ideas but you never know, it might work.) Or you could try the door of the nearest building, hope it's been left unlocked.

If you continue forward and charge into the group of zombies, turn to page 153.

If you stop and turn around in an attempt to catch the howlers off guard, proceed to page 155.

If, instead, you try to open one of the doors, turn to page 159.

Escape from Zombie Island

The man introduces himself as William. His wife, Helen, sits up front driving the van.

"We didn't leave town sooner," says William, "because we've been trying to find our daughter, Samantha. She went out to one of the local nightclubs early in the evening before all the madness began. We haven't heard from her since."

Helen says nothing as she guides the van along the rain dampened streets. Where she's going, you have no idea and right now you really couldn't care less. All that matters is that you're safe for the time being and able to relax. You've buckled yourself into a comfortable leather chair in the roomy, rear section of the van next to a small, round table attached to the floor. William sits across the table from you. There's a small couch behind you at the very back of the vehicle. How great would it be to lie down there for a little while and close your eyes? Although you know if you did you'd be asleep in a matter of minutes. *Probably not such a great idea under the circumstances.* So you sit there and listen to William talk, happy to have this time to recover from your recent exertions.

"We've been searching for hours," William tells you. "Trying to call her cell phone. No luck." You hear the concern in his tone. "We finally had to give up looking. The nightclub district's been overrun. The whole area's crawling with those damned... *things.*" You see him shake his head in the dim lighting of the van's interior. "*Zombies.* Hell, I don't know. Whatever you want to call them. Not to mention those screaming lunatics, attacking anyone they come across. One of them actually got his hands on Helen. That was the first one I had to shoot. The first one I had to kill…"

In the brief silence following this admission you hear the van accelerating over the wet pavement and the rain tapping at the roof over your head. William goes on to say that as much as it pains him and Helen, they have to look after themselves first and foremost at this point, try and find a way off the island, hope Samantha's able to do the same. "There's only so much looking we can do," he tells you. "It's too dangerous to keep at it any longer."

You feel bad for them. You've been pretty much on your own through all of this. It has to be a terrible thing having someone you

133

love unaccounted for with all that's going on.

"At least we found you," he says, forcing a smile onto his face. "God only knows what would have happened if we hadn't come along when we did. Where were you headed anyway?"

"I really don't know," you say. "I didn't even know where I was, exactly, when you showed up and saved my ass." You tell him the Cliffs Notes version of events leading up to this point: getting shot by the police officer… the surgery… escaping from the hospital...

He gives a low whistle. "I'm amazed you managed to stay on your feet as long as you did. Night like that has to take a lot out of a person."

"Yeah, I guess you could say that."

The longer you sit there the harder it is to keep your eyes open and your mind on the conversation.

"I tell you what," he says as he gets up from his chair. "I'm gonna head up front, keep Helen company for a while. You take it easy back here. If you happen to doze off we'll wake you up when we get there."

"Get where?"

A shrug. "Trying to figure that one out myself."

He climbs in between the two front seats and sits down on the passenger side.

Murmured conversation drifts back to you, mixes with the sounds of the rain and the road into a hypnotic blend of white noise.

Just need to rest my eyes. And then I'll be good to go.

As soon as you close your eyes, everything drifts away. The pain in your shoulder… The fear that's been a near constant companion throughout the evening…

Before long, sleep pulls you under.

And a jarring, roaring impact pulls you back out of it.

Total confusion. Darkness surrounds you as the world tilts violently back and forth. The seatbelt holding you into the chair keeps you from toppling to the floor. *What's going on?* you wonder in a near panic. *Where the hell am I?* And then it comes back to you. *William and Helen. The van.* Which leads you to the next logical question: Where, exactly, is the van?

"William? Helen?"

A wordless response from up front, barely audible over the

Escape from Zombie Island

constant roaring. It sounds like William but you can't be entirely sure. Has he been injured? *A good possibility*, you realize as water pools around your feet and you start to make some sense of the situation.

Somehow, impossible as it may seem, you realize the van has found its way into a river.

Next stop, bottom *of the river.*

You need to get out of here as quickly as you can. So far, all the windows have remained intact. It's easy to picture one of them breaking, though, and a torrent of water pouring into the van. You definitely do not want to be around when that happens.

After undoing your seatbelt, you stand up and brace your hands against the roof to keep from falling over. Your shoulder cries out against the move but you tell it to be quiet. This is life or death and a little pain is not going to stand between you and the former. You shouldn't have much of a problem opening the side door back here. All you have to do is find the handle in the dark, give it a pull and slide it open. Of course, as soon as you do that a whole lot of water will rush in. Not like it will matter to you after you've left the van and gone into the river. But what about William and Helen? Will they be able to find their way out? And will you be able to live with yourself if they can't, if you don't even try to help them?

If you decide you can't leave your rescuers behind, turn to page 161.

If you're convinced the only way you'll make it out of this van alive is by looking out for number one, proceed to page 163.

Ray Wallace

Escape from Zombie Island

$\longrightarrow \quad \longleftarrow$

"Thanks for everything," you say. "But I'm not getting out and walking around in this weather."

So the two of you exchange goodbyes and shortly thereafter you put the jeep in gear, drive up the rise and back toward town. You give your full attention to the road and the manual transmission as you haven't driven a stick in several years. You're happy you were able to drive away from the fallen tree without stalling out. There was a moment when the jeep bucked a little but you got it under control and kept moving forward. As you cruise along you try to figure out what you should do now. You definitely don't want to head back into town. Maybe you should go back to the hotel, find your cell phone and try to get in touch with someone who might be able to help you out. At least you'll be back on familiar ground. You have a weapon now too. The hotel might be the best place to spend the night and ride out the storm.

You wonder if and when the military will get involved, especially considering one of their own people started this whole mess to begin with. What had the pilot of that plane been up to anyway? Why did he have a canister filled with something so dangerous with him in the first place? Had he stolen it? Had it sprung a leak and transformed him into a howler mid-flight? Is that why the plane crashed?

Plenty of questions, to be sure. You wonder how soon it will be before you get any answers. If ever. You tell yourself you should probably stop letting your mind wander and pay more attention to the road. Getting into an accident, especially on a night like this, does not sound like your idea of a good time.

The windshield wipers whip back and forth as the road unspools before you. Now you have to try and remember the way back to the hotel. The only other time you've traveled this way was when you first arrived and the shuttle took you from the airport to your vacation destination.

And what a vacation it turned out to be.

But think of all the stories you'll be able to tell once you get back home. *If* you get back home.

Up ahead, the road branches off to the right. If you recall

137

correctly, the shuttle turned onto this new road before continuing onward to the hotel. And so you follow the long, gentle curve, drive a bit slower than you normally would, not wanting to take any chances in this weather. Eventually, you merge onto another four lane road. By now you're positive you're headed the right way. The hotel can't be more than a few minutes from here.

In the distance, a pair of yellow, flashing lights near the side of the road catches your attention. Hazard lights. Soon enough you see they belong to a red pickup truck with a black topper. Near the tailgate of the truck, a man waves his hands back and forth over his head, trying to get your attention.

"Just keep going," you say aloud, hoping that by hearing the words you might actually obey them. "This is no time to play Good Samaritan."

But then you think about Trent, stopping to rescue you from the howlers. And Natalie, taking you with her, letting you use her jeep when you didn't feel like accompanying her any further.

You slow the jeep, drive past the truck and pull over to the side of the road, back up and park in front of the other vehicle. As you sit there telling yourself this is a really stupid idea, the man appears at the driver's side window, looks in and smiles despite the rain pouring down on him. With a sigh you open the window.

"Car trouble?" you ask.

He nods his head. "Damn thing stalled and now it doesn't want to start up again."

The guy looks to be about thirty-five or so. He wears a navy blue t-shirt and a baseball cap with a logo on it you don't recognize, water pouring off the bill. "Been out here close to half an hour now. Didn't think anyone was ever going to stop." He gives you that smile again. "Sure glad someone did."

"Yeah, no problem," you say, trying to sound like you mean it. You tell him where you're headed. "I'd be willing to drop you off somewhere along the way. You shouldn't be out walking around in this weather, not with everything else that's going on."

"Well, that's awfully nice of you," he says before turning his head to the left then back to the right, as if checking to see if anyone else is around. For some reason, the way he does it gives you a bad feeling. When he reaches behind his back, pulls out a small but very

Escape from Zombie Island

serious looking pistol and points it at your face, that feeling gets a whole lot worse.

"Actually, I was thinking maybe you could let me have the jeep." His smile is nowhere to be found. "You see, I've got my little girl back there in the truck and I'm willing to do whatever it takes to get her somewhere safe."

You think about the gun Natalie gave you, now resting on the passenger seat, well within reach if you lean over and make a grab for it.

As if reading your mind the guy tells you, "Now don't go and do anything stupid."

So much for that idea. You sit there for a few seconds debating whether or not you should do as the guy says. Can he really be serious about shooting you? He's got his daughter with him, after all. She's probably sitting in the cab of the truck, watching this entire spectacle unfold. He couldn't possibly commit cold blooded murder with her looking on. Could he?

If you tell the guy it's not going to happen, that he needs to find someone else to carjack, turn to page 167.

If you decide you're better off letting him take the jeep as opposed to your life, proceed to page 169.

139

Ray Wallace

Escape from Zombie Island

———————————→ ←———————————

I've come this far. No point in turning back now.

"Alright, then," you tell her. "Let's do this."

She smiles and gives you a pat on the shoulder. "No matter what happens, we keep moving forward. If we work together and watch each other's backs then everything should be fine."

Without another word, she kills the engine, pulls the keys from the ignition, opens the driver's side door and hops out into the storm. You stick the gun down the front of your shorts then exit the vehicle, follow Natalie over to the fallen tree. Once again, she pushes her way into the space between a couple of branches. You do the same then watch as she climbs over the tree's thick trunk. After managing the same maneuver if a bit more clumsily, you emerge from the branches on the other side and make your way over to where Natalie waits at the side of the road.

"There, that wasn't so bad," she says and offers you a smile before turning and walking away. The storm goes about its business, a violent, angry thing, pouring rain and tossing lighting back and forth across the sky. *It will be a miracle if we don't get electrocuted.* Not something you can spend your time worrying about, though. All you can do is push onward and hope for the best.

Ten minutes pass without either of you saying a word. Not a single car approaches from the north. You can only hope this means people have decided to stay indoors, that there isn't a more sinister explanation for the lack of traffic.

Finally, to break the silence, you ask Natalie, "How long do you think it'll take us to get there?"

A shrug, visible in the light cast by a nearby streetlamp. "Half an hour, give or take."

So far, you've seen nothing but trees lining the road. You recall passing a collection of houses at one point when the shuttle took you from the airport to the hotel.

Where there are houses there will be people. And where there are people there could be—

Up ahead, a group of figures emerges from the darkness. Four, no, five of them heading your way at a leisurely pace. You stop but Natalie says, "Come on, we've got to keep moving." Not liking it but

141

not wanting to be left behind, you go after her. Maybe thirty seconds pass before two of the approaching figures let loose with screams that chill you more than the rain ever could. Then they take off running directly toward you. Natalie keeps walking. She has her gun in her hand, raises it and casually aims it toward the advancing figures.

"First shot to the chest," she says. "Bigger target. Hopefully it will slow them down. Second shot to the head."

Standing next to Natalie, you pull your gun out, check to make sure the safety's off. Using both hands to hold it steady, you take long, deep breaths and try to stay calm.

"Wait..." says Natalie.

Maybe twenty feet separates you from the howlers.

"Wait..."

The howlers get to within ten feet.

"Now!"

Natalie fires at the one on the left; you take the other one. The gun jumps in your hand but not as forcefully as you thought it might. Both howlers stagger as the bullets hit them. They don't stop coming at you though. You adjust your aim. *A little bit higher...* Fire again. A half second later Natalie fires too. Both howlers fall to the ground. They don't move.

Natalie gives you a little punch on the arm. "Nice shooting." She starts walking again, moves further out onto the blacktop, directly toward the other three figures. They continue to approach but much more slowly than the two you just put down. One of them looks like it's on the verge of losing its balance and falling over with every step it takes.

Definitely not howlers.

Zombies, then. You wait for Natalie to open fire but she surprises you by giving the zombies a wide berth and quickening her pace. The zombies stop, turn their heads and watch you go by, moaning all the while.

"Got to save our ammo," Natalie says by way of explanation. "No telling what might be waiting for us up ahead."

As the rain keeps pouring down, you try not to think about the fact that you shot and killed another human being. A sick and completely insane human being, yes, one hell-bent on making you

Escape from Zombie Island

sick and insane too. But a human being nonetheless.

Eventually, the houses you recall from the last time you passed this way come into view. A section of woods has been cleared to make room for this tiny neighborhood. No lights can be seen in any of the windows. Natalie wanders off the road toward one of the houses.

"Well, look what we've got here."

You follow as she cuts through the yard over to the porch where a mountain bike leans next to the front door.

"We can't take it," you tell her.

"And why not?"

"What if someone's still home? What if they need it?"

Before Natalie can respond, you approach the door and ring the buzzer.

"What are you doing?"

"If there's no one here then we can—"

Someone screams, no, *howls* from inside the house.

"Let's get out of here," says Natalie. She grabs the bike, carries it across the porch and pushes it through the yard. Just then the front door flies open and the howler, a woman, steps onto the porch, stands there screaming for all she's worth. Much to your horror, you hear the awful sound echoed by others of her kind as they emerge from within and behind the other houses.

Natalie curses and breaks into a run, pushing the bike beside her. Several howlers enter the road to the north, trying to keep you from escaping in that direction. More of them take to the street behind you, cutting off any chance of retreat.

Stay calm. Don't do anything stupid.

The way you see it you can stick with Natalie and try to shoot your way out of here or you can abandon the road, head toward the houses and the woods behind them, try to lose the howlers there and find a different route to the airport.

If you stick with Natalie and prepare to do some more shooting, turn to page 171.

If you think it's time for a different course of action and head for the woods, proceed to page 175.

143

Ray Wallace

Escape from Zombie Island

———————————→ ←———————————

No way are you going to risk getting a face full of the black gas. And so you hurry toward the dark hallway next to the DJ booth, manage to reach it without incident. Once inside the corridor, you see a glowing red exit sign at the far end near the ceiling. Halfway there you pass a pair of doors, one marked "Girls" and the other marked "Guys". You consider ducking into one of the bathrooms, hiding in one of the stalls for a while. But you decide against it, not wanting to be trapped in there if the nightclub gets completely overrun by hordes of the hungry dead. You'll be better off if you keep moving, try to find a way out of town and off this doomed island while you still have a chance.

You continue forward until you reach the unmarked door beneath the exit sign. Without hesitation, you place your hands on the push bar, give it a hard shove and step outside. To the left of the doorway you see a yellow dumpster. Directly before you, a small lot filled with cars. And beyond that an alleyway walled in by the backs of the buildings along the far side. Right now the area appears to be howler and zombie free. Of course, that could change so you do the only sensible thing and take off running into the stormy night.

The alleyway leads to a cross street which you follow, leaving the sounds of mayhem—the screams, the gunshots, the *boom* of something exploding—further behind. Houses with short driveways and single car garages line the road here. You think about stopping at one of them, seeing if anyone's home who might be able to help you out. But you decide against it wanting to put some more distance between yourself and the zombie horde terrorizing the downtown area behind you. So far, you've been fortunate to not run into any howlers. The few zombies you've seen have been avoided easily enough. One on one and with room to run, they haven't posed any real threat. You know better than to let your guard down, though. So you keep your head up and your eyes open, maintain a pace that shouldn't wear you out anytime soon.

Like going for a jog back home.

Good thing you made the decision to stay somewhat fit over the past few years. Cardio sure comes in handy when having to flee a zombie outbreak.

Ahead, you see an intersection with a four way stop. As you approach it, a car pulls up from the left and stops in front of you. Slowing to a walk, you start to go around the vehicle as the tinted passenger side window scrolls down and a man, leaning over from the driver's seat, asks if you need a lift.

Actually, you do need a lift but something about this situation doesn't feel right, like it's almost too good to be true. And the way the guy grins at you... Definitely something a bit creepy about it.

"I'm good," you tell him. "Thanks anyway."

"Really? Night like this? With everything that's going on out there?"

You wish the guy would roll up his window and drive off.

"Really. I'm fine."

Time to get out of here.

Once again, you begin circling the vehicle, ready to continue on your way. And that's when you feel a sharp, stinging sensation in the side of your neck. Cursing, you slap at the painful area, feel something small and thin and metallic stuck to the skin there. Pulling it free, you hold it up before your eyes and see what looks like a tiny dart complete with little feathers at its tail end.

"What the hell?"

The guy gets out of the car, lifts his hand up high enough so you can see the pistol he's holding over the vehicle's roof.

Dart gun, you realize.

"Nice shot, huh?" The grin still hasn't left his face. "It's true what they say... Practice does make perfect."

He walks around the car, casually, like he doesn't have a care in the world. And now you can see how big the guy is, bigger than any of the bouncers you saw shooting at zombies in front of the nightclub. You start to run but don't get far before your legs stop responding to your commands. Losing your balance, you fall to the sidewalk, landing hard enough to make a few bruises. You can only hope they end up being the worst of your injuries.

The guy laughs as you try to crawl away from him.

"Now where do you think you're going?"

You manage to make it a whole five feet or so before collapsing all the way to the ground. And there you lie as a feeling of complete paralysis settles into your arms and legs then throughout the rest of

Escape from Zombie Island

your body.

"Looks like you really do need a ride after all."

These words are the last thing you hear before the night crashes down on top of you and everything goes black...

Then:

Harsh, sterile light.

You blink against the sudden illumination as it settles in through your eyes and feeds the throbbing pain inside your head.

"Welcome back."

The guy who shot you with the dart gun leans into your field of vision.

"And how are we feeling?"

For the most part, the drug has worn off. You can move again although not very far. Leather straps hold you in place around your wrists, ankles and neck. As you lie there on your back, staring upward, you struggle against your restraints. It doesn't take you long to realize the futility of your actions.

"Where am I?" you ask, trying to stay calm.

"A place where no one will ever find you."

"What are you going to do?"

That weird grin of his returns.

"Something I've wanted to do for a long time now. And on a night like this, with everyone on the island a bit preoccupied..." He shows you the knife in his hand. It looks particularly sharp. "It was an opportunity I couldn't pass up."

What you wouldn't give to be back outside among the zombies and the howlers instead of in here with this monster. At least out there you've got a fighting chance. But, as the saying goes: that's the way the cookie crumbles.

THE END

Escape from Zombie Island

———————————→ ←———————————

Before you can even consider the possible consequences of your actions, you turn and throw yourself at the bartender's assailant. After tackling the infected lunatic to the floor, you roll away and scramble to your feet.

"Let's go," you say and grab the bartender by the elbow, ready to guide her the rest of the way across the dance floor toward the hallway next to the DJ booth. Just then, however, a pair of howlers steps into your path, effectively blocking any further progress. "Oh, great."

The bartender pulls against your grip.

"This way," she says.

Releasing her arm, you follow her back toward the bar, circle around behind it, past the rows of bottles and the long mirror mounted to the wall with the Guinness logo on it. Maybe ten feet beyond the mirror she stops, places her hands against a section of the wall and pushes. To your surprise the wall gives way revealing a doorway you had no idea was even there. Without a word she ducks inside; a second later, you do the same.

"Close it," she says.

You shut the door, muffling the cacophony of the club's main room. Within moments someone begins pounding on it from the outside. The bartender flips a light switch on the wall then reaches past you and slides the deadbolt into place, locking the door.

"Don't know how long that will hold them," she says.

Looking around, you see you're in a storage room. A lone light bulb glows high above you near the ceiling. Discarded nightclub fixtures fill much of the room. There: several square, metal tables pushed against one of the walls, a dozen or so metal chairs standing on top of them. There: a marquee sign that may have been attached to the front of the building at some point, random black letters attached to its face, too few to convey any sort of coherent message. And there: what looks like an electric cooler, seven or eight feet long, its metal surface dully reflecting the light from above.

The bartender walks over to one end of the cooler and pulls it away from the wall.

"Here, help me move this."

The cooler's on wheels so it doesn't take long for the two of you to roll the heavy fixture up against the door. Kneeling down, the bartender uses the small levers near the wheels to lock them into place. You do the same on your side.

"That might keep them out for a while," she says.

"What now?" you wonder aloud.

"Now we go up."

The bartender heads toward a black, spiral staircase near the back of the room. As she climbs, the metal stairs clang beneath her boots. Again, you follow her lead. When you reach the top you step onto a short landing at the far end of which you see a doorway set into the wall. The bartender opens the door and steps through. You hear the sounds of the storm and the city as you make your way out into the rainy night.

The two of you walk the twenty or so feet to the edge of the roof, past the massive AC housing to a spot almost directly above the club's front entrance. And then you look down.

Figures dash across the street and along both sidewalks. In all the confusion it's often hard to tell who's being chased and who's doing the chasing. To your left, a minivan slams into a parked car near the side of the road and gets swarmed by a crowd of the walking dead. To your right, flames leap from the windows along the front of a building, black smoke billowing toward the sky. A couple of cars burn too, one of them in the middle of the street. The rain appears to have little to no effect on the flames. Several car alarms blare incessantly. From the direction of the police station you hear sirens and the sound of somebody firing an automatic weapon.

A piercing scream draws your attention to the other side of the street directly in front of you where a woman stands before the entrance of a restaurant. Two figures—zombies, it would seem—stand to either side of her. They've got her by the wrists, holding her arms out wide in some strange parody of a crucifixion. From behind the woman, a zombie leans in and bites into the side of her neck. Even at this distance you can see the blood pouring out of the wound.

"My God," says the bartender from where she stands next to you. "What is this? The end of the world?"

"Maybe not the world," you tell her, shaking your head. "It's the

150

Escape from Zombie Island

end of something though."

A few minutes later, the two of you head back to the landing inside the doorway.

"By the way, my name is Callie," says the bartender as the two of you stand there staring out into the rain and the darkness.

"Good to meet you, Callie," you say. "I only wish it could have been under better circumstances."

"Let's hope they don't get any worse."

"I'm sure the troops are on their way," you tell her, trying to sound like you actually believe it. "Someone has to clean up this mess."

You pass the time exchanging small talk with Callie and listening to the mayhem consuming the city, wondering if either of you will actually get out of this place alive. At some point, you realize the pounding on the door below has stopped.

"There's something I need to get," Callie tells you and, without another word, heads downstairs. You watch from your elevated vantage point as she crosses the room and moves the cooler out of the way. She then presses her ear up against the door before opening it and stepping through.

You feel a surge of relief when, less than a minute later, she walks back into the room. After closing and locking the door once again, she pushes the cooler back into place and heads for the stairs. When she reaches the landing she shows you what she brought with her.

"A bottle of bourbon?" you ask.

"The good stuff," she tells you with a smile. "Top shelf."

While opening the bottle, she tells you the club is crawling with zombies. "None of those screamers though."

She takes a swig of bourbon, hands the bottle over to you. The first swallow makes you cough. After a few more the anxiety you've felt throughout most of the evening subsides a little. A couple more and you actually start to relax.

By the time the sun comes out, the bottle's contents have noticeably diminished. If you live through all of this, you're sure to have one serious hangover.

"Looks like the rain finally stopped," says Callie.

Squinting against the morning light, you wander a bit unsteadily out through the doorway and approach the edge of the roof. Looking

151

down toward the street, you see a completely different scene than the one that greeted you the last time you were here. No more howlers. No more terrified people running around. Just…

Zombies.

They fill the street for as far as you can see in either direction, wandering around aimlessly for the most part. Groups of them huddle together in rough circles—feeding, no doubt. As you watch, a few of them stop what they're doing and look up toward you. Now you can hear them, a low, collective moaning rising from below. It's the only sound you hear until…

Boom…

Boom…

BOOM…

Like a giant's footsteps, somewhere in the distance, growing progressively louder. In the skies north of the city, a pair of jet fighters comes into view. Billowing clouds of dust and debris rise up from the ground, each larger than the one preceding it the closer they get.

"What are they…" Callie says as the fighters roar by overhead, dropping their bombs and laying waste to the strip, wiping out all those zombies.

And, unfortunately, taking you out with them.

THE END

Escape from Zombie Island

⟶   ⟵

Here goes nothing, you say to yourself and run directly toward the waiting zombies. There has to be a good dozen of them between you and the end of the alleyway. And it's going to take some fancy footwork to get past them all.

From behind you, the howlers cry out. You know it's going to be tough to shake them once you've made your way past the zombies. One problem at a time, though. First you have to deal with the creatures that want to eat you. Then you'll deal with the ones that want to infect you.

As you reach the pack of zombies, the first two—a young man in a tattered football jersey and a woman with some awful looking burn marks on the side of her face—reach toward you, the halfhearted gestures of the dead, too late to grab you as you go running by. You have to slow your pace a little as you juke to the left then to the right, pull off a rather impressive spin move to free yourself from the clutches of a particularly eager dead woman. After side stepping two more zombies, you stiff arm another one out of the way. And now only a few more of the undead stand between you and the mostly empty alleyway beyond.

As you prepare to execute another move that would make an NFL running back jealous, your foot comes down on something hard and rounded—a rock or broken chunk of asphalt—and you roll the same ankle you injured only a short while ago. The flash of pain causes your leg to buckle and you fall, smacking your left elbow against the unforgiving surface of the alleyway in the process. You struggle back to your feet, well aware of what will happen if you don't keep moving. A valiant effort, to be sure, but your injuries slow you down enough to allow several sets of hands to grab hold of you.

And that's when you make a rather interesting discovery: The zombies are stronger than you imagined they would be. Try as you might, you can't fight your way free of them. More hands grab you, more dead bodies press in around you. As the biting and the clawing begin, you lash out, fighting back against your undead assailants, all to no avail.

What a terrible way to end your vacation. As the saying goes, timing is everything. And it certainly looks like your timing could have been better when you planned this little island getaway.

THE END

Escape from Zombie Island

⟶ ⟵

You stop and pivot on your good ankle then run directly toward the pursuing howlers. It's one of those crazy moves you hope might catch them off guard, maybe confuse them enough for you to get past them and out of this alleyway.

Unfortunately, it doesn't quite work out that way.

The lead howler, a tall, lanky fellow with a buzz cut and a dark goatee, lowers his shoulder and takes you down with a textbook football tackle. You land flat on your back on the pavement, the air rushing out of you in a great *whoosh*. As you struggle to catch your breath, your assailant sits on top of you, straddling you, head cocked to one side as he watches you, seemingly curious despite the madness burning in his eyes.

A minute or so passes before you can breathe somewhat normally again. During that time the other howlers have gathered around, stand there staring down at you. All the while the sound of moaning has grown louder as the pack of zombies draws closer, ever closer...

Without warning, the howler holding you down leans in close and exhales a cloud of black gas, obscuring the sight of the alleyway around you and the nighttime sky overhead. Caught off guard, you breathe it in.

The gas burns its way down your throat and into your lungs. The pain spreads quickly along the nerves spanning the entirety of your body. It's an agony beyond imagining, one that consumes you, causes you to lose all sense of who you are, of even *what* you are. All you know is this terrible, unendurable pain that's taken hold of you, mind, body and soul. It's what you've become, a thrashing, screaming incarnation of all the pain in the world distilled to its finest essence. Surely, nothing can survive this level of torment.

Please let it end.

And, eventually, it does end.

Not with death, no, but with a transformation.

You are a host now, enslaved to a need you find impossible to deny or resist. As the world shifts back into focus around you, a hand reaches down and grabs you by the arm, helps lift you to your feet. And now you stand face to face with your assailant, the one who infected you. He releases his grip, throws his head back and *howls*. You mimic him, relishing the feel of the sound as it rushes up through your throat and escapes into the night. An expression of pure, wordless desire and rage. A sensation like a mild electrical current travels throughout your body and with it an overriding imperative ordering you to *move*, to find other potential hosts and infect them *now*.

And so, in the company of your new howler friends, you take off running into the night. People cry out at your approach. Some of them carry weapons. You take a bullet in the leg. A knife scrapes across your ribcage. But it doesn't matter. The pain of these injuries is a minor thing, instantly forgotten. All that matters is the feeling driving you onward, demanding you offer the gift of the black gas to any potential host that crosses your path.

And that's exactly what you do.

For an hour you lead your own personal rampage throughout the city streets, manage to pass the infection along to half a dozen people in that time. But then the electricity crackling inside of you dissipates. The crying woman you have pinned up against the wall of a building manages to escape. You want to chase her, to hunt her down, to breathe into her this new life that's taken you over but a sudden lethargy overwhelms you. The electricity fizzles out. You drop to your knees as all the strength flows out of your body before collapsing all the way down to the ground. A deep and impenetrable darkness flows into you. And there you die.

But you don't stay dead. Not completely.

The darkness dissipates as a hunger beyond imagining forces a moan from your lips.

You sit up. Look around. Push yourself to your feet. And just then a man runs into you causing the two of you to collapse in a tangled heap.

"Get off of me!" he screams.

You bite into his throat. After a few more bites he falls silent and stops moving. Others of your kind, other zombies, gather round, kneel down and tear at the man's clothes, partake of the feast offered by his flesh. When only scraps remain, you stand and walk away, the hunger satiated.

But not for long.

Escape from Zombie Island

As the hours drift by the numbers of the undead continue to grow. You and your fellow zombies hunt in packs, finding it easier to first surround your prey and cut off any means of escape. After each feeding, the hunger diminishes and you feel a sense of calm as it relinquishes its control over you. But the feeling is an ephemeral thing. Before long, you start moaning again and growling deep in your throat. No matter how much you eat, the hunger inside of you wants more, always more.

How much is enough? some deep, hidden part of you that may have once been human can't help but wonder. *Will it ever be enough?*

Finally, the night starts to fade as the sun fills the city streets with morning light. With the dawn you hear something strange over the collective moaning of your fellow zombies: a low booming from outside the city, growing progressively louder, like giant footsteps drawing nearer. The storm covering the island throughout the night has finally moved on leaving behind mostly clear skies—only a few lingering clouds drift by overhead. Unexpected movement draws your attention toward those clouds.

There!

Two airplanes out of the north. They drop their bombs, one after the next. You stand and watch as the resulting explosions draw ever closer until the ground beneath your feet trembles. A building maybe a hundred feet away erupts in a cloud of fire, dust and debris, raining chunks of brick and shards of glass down onto the street. The next explosion leaves a smoking crater in the middle of the road. And the one after that…

THE END

Ray Wallace

Escape from Zombie Island

⟶　←

You head for the nearest doorway, grab the handle and hope for a miracle. And look at that! It opens.

Hurrying into the building, you pull the door closed and locate the deadbolt, slide it into place as one of the howlers slams up against the outside of the door. You hear it screaming out there, pounding on the door with its fists. And speaking of pounding... Your heart feels as though it might jump out of your chest. Talk about your close calls! Standing there, you examine your new surroundings while trying to decide what your next move should be.

It's mostly dark in here but enough light drifts in through an open doorway across the room to let you take in your surroundings. You're in a rectangular space, maybe twenty feet long by a dozen wide, a storage area for some sort of retail establishment. Shelves loaded with boxes of various sizes line the walls. More boxes stand in neat stacks on the floor next to a table with papers scattered across its surface.

The pounding on the door behind you continues. Then:

"Daddy! Daddy! One of them got in!"

You see a child-sized silhouette in the lighted doorway, there one instant and gone the next.

Another voice, deeper and noticeably slurred: "Damn it. I told you to double check the door, make sure it was locked."

A rather large man steps into the doorway, arm outstretched and pointed in your direction.

As you open your mouth to tell him you're not one of them, not one of the infected and definitely not one of those walking dead things, he pulls the trigger of the gun in his hand, once, twice, three times in rapid succession. And, despite the fact that he sounds like he's been drinking, his aim is true. The first bullet catches you in the stomach, the next two in the chest, throwing you against the door. You slide down to the floor, all the strength flowing out of you much like the blood flowing from your wounds. The man walks across the room, gun hanging at his side, stands there staring down at you.

"I'm not gonna let you hurt my boy," he says in a low tone, almost growling the words. "You hear me? Not any of you."

As he raises the gun and points it at your face, you want tell him you'd never do anything to hurt his boy. But you can't form the words. Not that it would do you much good at this point anyway. That pistol of his inflicted some serious damage. He's probably doing you a favor when he pulls the trigger one last time.

THE END

Escape from Zombie Island

$\longrightarrow$ $\longleftarrow$

You make your way toward the front of the van, place your hands on the headrests of the seats and lean forward. In the moonlight you can make out the silhouettes of William and his wife where they sit. You reach out and grab William by the shoulder, give him a shake, nearly losing your balance in the process.

"William?"

He says something incomprehensible, clearly shaken up by whatever accident brought the three of you here. Trying to elicit any sort of response from Helen proves to be a fruitless endeavor. You feel the seconds ticking by, fully aware each one brings you that much closer to dying in here. Somehow, you have to get William and his wife out of their seats and back to the sliding door. After that...

There's only so much I can do.

Once you open that door everyone will have to fend for themselves.

You manage to find and disengage the buckle holding William's seatbelt in place. When he slumps forward you grab him by the shoulder, give him a rough shake while shouting his name. This time, to your relief, he responds:

"What... what's going on?"

"Come on, William," you say. "We have to get out of here. Now!"

You undo Helen's seatbelt, hoping she'll come around. *Probably smacked her head when the van plunged into the river.* With your bad shoulder and the unsteadiness of your surroundings, there's no way you'll be able to get her out of her seat and into the back of the van on your own.

"William, I need your help."

The fact that the van hasn't filled up with water by now seems like a miracle. Swirling black waves rush over the hood and obscure what little light enters through the windshield. Now you feel a real sense of panic. Time is running out. The van could go under at any moment.

"William!"

He reaches for Helen, tries to move her but everything's happening much too slowly.

161

Should've gotten out while I could.

If you turn and leave right now you can get to the side door, throw it open and take your chances in the river. With any luck, William and Helen will be able to escape too. You try to convince yourself you've done enough here, more than a lot of people ever would.

If you don't leave now you never will.

As you push away from the pair of seats you've been holding onto, the driver's side window gives way in an implosion of glass and water. The front end of the van sinks even further, nearly pitching you forward into the dashboard.

Screw this.

You turn and lunge toward the back of the van as William shouts his wife's name over and over. Falling to the floor, you crawl across the wet carpeting toward the door where you reach out blindly, desperately trying to locate the handle. Behind you, another window implodes while you continue running your hands over the door.

There!

You grab the handle and give it a pull, sliding the door open as far as you can. Water rushes in through the opening, knocking you back against the base of the table. The van fills up rapidly now, rocks back and forth with even greater intensity. The water rises over your calves then past your knees. In a move of sheer desperation, you fight your way over to the door and prepare to pull yourself through when something grabs you by the leg.

William!

Totally off balance, you manage to take a deep breath before you plunge into the water filling the front half of the van. William has both hands wrapped around your leg now, holding on for dear life. You try to kick at him in the enclosed space with your free leg but he doesn't let go. Before long, what strength you have left after all you've been through disappears as does any chance of making it out of here alive. The darkness presses in on all sides.

So this is how it ends.

At least you can take some solace in the fact that you tried to do the right thing.

THE END

Escape from Zombie Island

———————————→ ←———————————

"Sorry, William. Sorry, Helen." Empty words, you know, but it's all you have to offer.

You move over to the door. It doesn't take you very long to locate the handle. Not wanting to waste any more time, you give it a pull and slide the door open. Water surges in, nearly knocking you off your feet.

It's going to be fine, everything's going to be fine.

With that, you take a deep breath and lunge through the open doorway into the dark and turbulent waters of the river.

The current pulls you under, tumbling you end over end, causing you to lose all sense of direction. When your hand brushes against a rock you orient yourself, press your feet against the river's floor and push upward with all the strength you can muster. Your lungs start to burn as you ascend through the blackness surrounding you in all directions.

Almost there.

You hope it's true, *need* it to be true, knowing you won't be able to hold your breath much longer.

Breaking the surface of the water, you desperately suck in air as you kick your legs and paddle your arms, look around wildly for some sign of the river's edge, any promise of salvation. Enough moonlight sifts through the clouds high overhead for you to see the foaming caps of the waves undulating all around you, the dark outlines of trees along the bank of the river a good thirty feet away.

You swim, pausing long enough to kick free of your slippers, knowing you'll cover more distance without them. And you do. The trees draw nearer, ever nearer as the river effortlessly carries you along. Instead of fighting the current you go with it, slowly make your way toward shallow water. Finally, with the last of your strength threatening to desert you, your feet touch bottom. Soon after, you crawl out of the water and onto the muddy ground at the river's edge.

A little further… Just a little bit more…

The words echo inside your head as you make your way up the slope of the bank, coughing and breathing heavily all the while. When you reach the roots near the base of a tree you stop, roll over onto your back, stare upward into the leaves and the branches blocking out much of the sky above. The rain continues to fall, dripping down onto your face and the exposed skin of your arms and feet.

Sitting up, you look toward the river, its waters churning and bloated by the healthy offering of rain from the heavens. How in the world did the van end up in there? You imagine a bridge, weakened by the storm, collapsing as the van drove onto it. Or maybe the bridge had been sabotaged. Could a group of howlers have been responsible? Are they smart enough, coordinated enough to undertake such an enterprise? Chances are you'll never know the answers to these questions. Right now you're happy you can still ask them. Good thing you got out of the van when you did.

If I'd stuck around and tried to rescue William and Helen, things would have turned out much differently.

You can't help but feel guilty, though, about leaving them behind. Closing your eyes, you try to clear your mind of those final images from inside the van. As you do, a sudden fatigue washes over you like the waters of the river, dark and unrelenting. The pain in your shoulder reminds you of other hardships faced throughout the evening. You can only wonder at how many more you'll have to endure before the night is through.

Despite the wet and the cold, you lie down on the ground, needing to relax for a few minutes, long enough to regain some of your strength before moving on.

Just a few minutes...

Before you know it, the sounds of the rain and the river conspire to pull you under. Once again, having reached the limits of your endurance, you give in to the lure of slumber, grateful to escape the world if only for a while.

And so you sleep.

Until...

Light, leaking in through your eyelids... The sensation of something tugging at your leg... Something else pulling at your arm...

You open your eyes as agony explodes throughout various points of your body. Crying out, you sit up, kick and punch at the group of vacant eyed people kneeling around you, biting and pulling

Escape from Zombie Island

at the flesh of your leg, your arm, your face. Fueled by pain and horror, you almost tear yourself free of them, almost make it to your feet and escape.

Almost.

But not quite.

Instead, the zombies drag you back down to the ground as more of their kind arrive on the scene and join the party. Looking around, you see the hunger in their faces, those awful faces. You also see the morning has dawned bright and clear. The rain has stopped and the river has calmed. In a nearby tree a bird sings a lovely little tune. It looks like it's shaping up to be a beautiful day. Too bad all these walking, hungry corpses had to show up and ruin it.

THE END

Ray Wallace

Escape from Zombie Island

"I don't think so," you tell the guy despite the fact that he's got a gun pointed at your face. "There's no way I'm going to let you strand me out here."

Beneath the bill of that baseball cap, the smile returns although it doesn't look quite as friendly as before. It comes across as more of a sneer, actually.

"Last chance," he says as the rain continues to fall. A car whizzes by without slowing. "Get out of the vehicle."

You sit there, silent and unmoving. Lightning flashes and as the ensuing thunder dies the guy says, "Okay, then. If that's the way it has to be..."

He pulls the trigger.

Looks like he wasn't bluffing after all.

THE END

Ray Wallace

Escape from Zombie Island

———————————————————→ ←———————————————————

"Alright. Fine."

The guy steps aside as you open the door.

"That's right, nice and slow," he says as you exit the vehicle. He circles around behind you and sticks the gun in the small of your back. "Move."

You walk alongside the jeep toward the pickup truck with its blinking hazard lights. Two cars go by, tires kicking up water, some of it splashing your legs. As you pass the cab of the truck, you look through the driver's side window, see a diminutive figure sitting there, wide eyes reflecting the scant light making its way inside. The gun presses into you a bit more forcefully.

"Keep moving."

At the rear of the truck the guy unlatches the tailgate and the back of the topper, tells you to get in. You do as instructed, finding it nice to be out of the rain again even after such limited exposure to the storm. If only it was under better circumstances.

"We'll be leaving now," says the guy, still aiming the gun at you. "So sit tight and don't do anything stupid."

He closes the tailgate, lowers the topper door back into place and latches it shut. As the rain pounds on the plastic roof over your head, you wonder what you'll do now that you're stranded here without a vehicle. None of your options strike you as very appealing. At least you managed to avoid getting shot. As bad as your current situation may seem, it could definitely be a whole lot worse.

From up front you hear the sound of one of the doors *thunk*ing shut. Turning your head, you look through the window separating the bed and the cab of the truck, see no sign of the little girl. Staring out through the windshield, you watch as eventually the jeep pulls onto the road and drives off into the stormy night.

Turning from the window, you sit there for a few minutes, trying to decide upon a course of action. The way you see it you really only have two options from which to choose.

Option number one: You can get out of the truck and walk through the rain, try to hitch a ride the rest of the way to the hotel.

Or option number two: You can sit tight and wait for the storm to let up before setting off.

Ray Wallace

Either way, you should try to find a weapon of some sort in case you run afoul of some howlers or another individual like the one who just carjacked you. There's certainly nothing back here that could help you out in a fight. What about up front? A tire iron maybe?

Worth checking out.

You only hope the guy who stole Natalie's jeep left the door to the cab unlocked when he left with his daughter.

If you decide to leave immediately and continue the journey to the hotel on foot, go to page 177.

If you think it wiser to stay where you are for a while, proceed to page 181.

Escape from Zombie Island

She's gotten me this far. No point in abandoning her now.

While you run, you point the gun at the nearest howler and pull the trigger. Natalie manages to squeeze off a few shots of her own while pushing the bike. Three howlers go down. You wound two others but they keep coming after you, if a bit slower. Natalie tells you to get on the bike.

"Sit on the handlebars."

You do as your told, bracing your feet on the front forks as Natalie hops on behind you and starts pedaling for all she's worth.

The two of you race across the wet blacktop, the rain stinging your face. When you glance back over your shoulder and see the pursuing howlers falling steadily back, you laugh out loud from sheer exhilaration. Natalie pedals hard for a while, swerving around the occasional zombie along the way. A scary moment occurs when she almost loses control of the bike, barely manages to keep it upright as the two of you continue onward through the night and the ever falling rain.

Eventually, the airport tower comes into view.

About fifty feet from the road you see the dark strip of the airport's main runway. The four story tower sits at the far end, a white light blinking steadily at the top. Next to the tower squats the dark bulk of the airport terminal. A string of white lights glows along the middle of the runway. You see another light, too, blinking near the base of the tower. And this particular light is moving.

"An airplane!" you shout.

Natalie guides the bike over to the side of the road, onto the wet grass there toward the more forgiving terrain of the runway. On several occasions a wreck seems imminent. But, again, Natalie manages to keep the bike upright as she pedals across the slick grass. As you watch, the small plane taxis into position as it prepares for takeoff. Before it can do so, however, Natalie steers the bike across the runway and up next to the plane where you jump off, waving your arms and shouting, "Stop! Wait! Wait!"

The plane stops.

Natalie pushes the bike off the runway then the two of you circle around the plane to the door, sealed shut in anticipation of takeoff.

You step forward and bang on the door with your fist then move back as it opens and a small staircase lowers to the ground. Without further prompting, the two of you enter the waiting aircraft.

The plane holds six rows of seats, four seats per row, a narrow aisle dividing them down the middle, about half of them occupied by fellow passengers. A man wearing a white button down shirt and black pants stands in the open doorway leading to the cockpit. He holds a gun in his right hand, pointed in your general direction.

"What? You think any of those maniacs could ride a bike like that?" asks Natalie.

"No, actually, I don't." The guy lowers the gun. "Had to be sure though. Nice to have you on board. We'll be taking off shortly. Now find some seats and buckle yourselves in."

With that he turns and disappears through the doorway. You head toward the back of the plane, nodding to the other passengers along the way. The last row is unoccupied so you and Natalie sit there along either side of the aisle. As soon as your seatbelt clicks into place the airplane starts to roll forward. Rain lashes at the small oval of a window to your left, covers the glass in tiny rivulets of water. A brief flash of lightning illuminates the darkness, there and gone in an instant.

The whirring of the engines grows louder as the plane gathers speed, gently pushing you back in your seat. The idea of leaving the island excites you, of course, but the size of the plane and the weather do make you a bit nervous. The plane continues to accelerate until, finally, the nose tilts upward and the wheels lose contact with the ground. Now it's only a short flight to the mainland.

We'll be there in no time.

Looks like you were right to stick with Natalie after all.

A minute into the flight, people noticeably relax. You hear murmured conversation from those seated in front of you. Natalie looks across the aisle at you, offers a smile.

"I guess we timed that pretty much perfectly."

You smile in return. "Yeah, I guess you could say that."

The two of you talk for a little while, mostly about what the military should do about the situation on the island. Natalie thinks they may have to bomb it, write the whole place off. "Too many casualties if you send in ground troops." Then she falls silent,

Escape from Zombie Island

apparently distracted, shifting her gaze and staring at something behind you. After unbuckling her safety belt, she stands and says, "Excuse me," then pushes past you toward the window on your side of the plane.

"What is it?" you ask.

She doesn't respond, keeps staring out the window, captivated by something out there.

"Natalie?"

Eventually, she moves out of the way, motions for you to take a look. At first, you don't know what you're looking for and then you see it: a blinking light, out there in the darkness, disappearing as lightning cuts its way across the sky before reappearing again.

"Another plane," says Natalie.

"How far?"

"Hard to tell." A pause. "Close though. Less than a mile."

"Who do you think—"

Before you even finish the question you have your answer. A new light source streams away from the other aircraft, races out in front of it, turns and heads your way.

"I had a feeling something like this might happen. Guess they can't take any chances with this thing getting out."

So close and yet so far…

You turn from the window and lean back in your seat. Natalie relaxes in the seat next to you, reaches up and puts her hand on your shoulder.

"Well, it was nice knowing you."

"Yeah, you too."

A few seconds pass before an explosion of light and heat and a mighty roar consumes the interior of the airplane.

And then there's nothing.

Nothing at all.

THE END

Ray Wallace

Escape from Zombie Island

$\longrightarrow$ $\longleftarrow$

You turn and run toward the house across the highway, heading for the open space between it and the house next door. A single howler stands in your way, easily dispatched with a shot from your trusty little handgun. When you reach the other side of the road, Natalie yells for you to stop, to come back. But you don't stop, you don't go back. Instead, you keep running as a collective screech goes up from a number of other howlers. Looking back, you see three of them have decided to give chase. You pass alongside the house and enter the back yard, nearly fall on the wet grass next to an above ground swimming pool but manage to maintain your balance. Now it's only ten feet or so to the front line of trees at the back of the yard. Beyond that lies nothing but forest, plenty thick enough in this lighting to lose anyone who might try to follow you.

As you move past the front line of trees, you slow your pace to more of a jog. The last thing you need is to run face first into a low branch or step into a hole and snap your ankle. Your eyes adjust to the deepening gloom as you push your way further into the woods. Eventually, you stop and hide behind a tree where you listen for sounds of pursuit. A howler screams, a fairly distant sound from somewhere further off in the woods. Then there's nothing but the rattling of the rain on the leaves and a low rumble of thunder.

Breathing a sigh of relief, you stay where you are for a couple of minutes wanting to make absolutely certain the immediate vicinity is howler free. And then you step away from the tree, set off in what you're pretty sure is a northerly direction, wanting to make your way back to the road and continue on to the airport. You hope Natalie escaped the howler ambush. With any luck, you'll run into her again and the two of you can still leave the island together. You know you can make her understand why you did what you did, why you left her like that. And if not... At least you'll both still be alive.

You step on something that feels like an old, soggy tree branch. But then it does something no tree branch ever would—it moves, twisting and sliding from beneath your foot. The thing rises up, a black silhouette against the darkness of the forest floor. And then it lunges at you. Pain explodes below your left knee. Another lunge and another spike of agony, this one directly above the ankle. You kick at the moving shadow and it slithers off through the grass and the wet leaves that litter the ground.

No, no, no, no, no...

You limp away from the scene of the attack, arrows of white hot pain shooting through your leg every time you put weight on it. So you eluded the howlers only to be bitten by a snake! A poisonous one, too, judging by the severity of the attack. In desperation you stop and tear a strip of cloth from the bottom of your shirt, tie it around your leg as tightly as you can above the knee, hope it can prevent the venom from spreading into the rest of your body. And then you continue onward through the woods.

A few minutes later, you realize you have no idea which direction you're headed. Presumably north but you can't be sure. And then it dawns on you that you don't really care. You feel tired all of a sudden, your legs increasingly heavy, requiring more effort to move them with every step you take. Sitting down among the roots of a particularly large tree, you lean back against the coarse skin of its trunk.

You have to keep moving! a voice yells inside your head. Easier said than done, though. A growing numbness replaces the pain in your leg before spreading throughout the rest of your body. Each time you pull in a breath it feels like more of an effort as does the simple act of sitting upright. And so you lean over and fall to the wet ground, water dripping down on you from the leaves and branches overhead. You want to sleep now, right here on the forest floor. A quick little nap, that's all. You can press on and find Natalie after you wake up. Yeah, now there's a great idea. Except for one small problem.

You don't wake up.

THE END

Escape from Zombie Island

————————————→ ←————————————

You know you have to keep moving. If the situation worsens—and you see no reason why it wouldn't—and the zombie-slash-howler population continues to grow, it might only be a matter of time before a sizable horde of said zombies-slash-howlers makes its way here. And a member of that horde may be inquisitive enough to investigate your little hiding place in the back of the truck. Of course, there's always a chance someone might come along and rescue you. Not a very good chance, though. Presumably, everyone on the island has their own problems they have to deal with by now. If you want to find a way out of this situation you'll have to do it on your own. And that will involve making your way back to familiar territory.

You open the tailgate then raise the back of the topper before climbing out into the rain again. Hurrying around to the driver side door, you grab the handle and give it a pull. The door pops open and the interior light turns on.

"Yes!"

Not wasting any time, you look behind the truck's bench seat, find the tire iron on the floor held in place by a metal clip. Grabbing it, you heft the weight of the metal bar, satisfied you now have a passable weapon in your possession. Stepping back, you close the door then turn and walk along the side of the road toward the hotel.

It can't be more than a couple of miles from here.

Moving at a brisk walk you should be there in half-an-hour, forty-five minutes at the most.

You hum a meandering melody as you slog along through the grass a few feet from the edge of the road. Cars go by on occasion, none of them bothering to slow down. Lightning flashes intermittently followed by deep roars of thunder. All in all, you can think of a thousand or so other places you'd rather be right now.

Aside from running across a few random zombies which you manage to avoid, the journey passes uneventfully. With the rain still falling, you arrive at the roundabout in front of the hotel. Looking around for signs of howlers, you listen for the telltale sounds of their screams. Nothing. Besides the steady hiss of the rain and the wind rustling the leaves of nearby palm trees, the place is quiet. Too quiet.

Ray Wallace

The fact that the hotel looks to be without power, stands there dark and lifeless before you, only adds to the feeling of trepidation slowly but surely building inside of you. But you've come this far. No point in turning back now. Besides, where else would you go? Isn't it why you came here in the first place? Because you have nowhere else to go?

You walk across the asphalt circle over to the hotel entrance, passing two parked cars along the way. Approaching the glass doorway, you take a deep breath to steady your nerves then open the door and step through, mentally preparing yourself for whatever might await you inside.

Aside from the dim glow cast by a couple of emergency lights—one over near the elevator doors and one at the mouth of the hallway leading back to the rooms on this floor—darkness infuses the lobby. You stand in the middle of the room, tire iron held at your side, trying to decide on your next move. And that's when you hear it. A low sound. Barely audible. Like something or someone in the throes of pain. Or pleasure. Or both.

Moaning.

It emanates from behind the check-in counter, the person responsible ducked down and out of sight.

"Hello?" you say just loud enough to be heard by whoever—or *what*ever—is hiding back there. Maybe it's someone who's been injured and needs your help.

"*Hello.*" This time you say it a bit louder.

The moaning continues and now you see movement as a hand reaches up to grab the edge of the countertop. A rather filthy hand, by the looks of it. Bloody? More movement now as the person's head rises up into view. First you see the blonde, matted hair followed by the eyes, wide and staring. Lifeless. By the time the woman's entire face comes into view you're not all that surprised to see a red, gritty substance smeared across her lips. Mouth open, she chews on what looks like a strip of raw flesh.

The dead woman stands fully upright, turns and walks toward the end of the counter. You take a step back toward the entranceway, ready to head out into the storm once again. Apparently, returning to this place wasn't such a great idea after all.

Back to the drawing board.

Escape from Zombie Island

Before you can leave the hotel, two men and a woman push their way through the entranceway and into the lobby. Then one of the men starts to *howl*...

You take off running past the counter and down the hallway, the emergency lights providing sufficient illumination to guide your way. The howlers give chase. You run all the way to the end of the hallway, push through the emergency exit and into the stairwell beyond...

And directly into a crowd of the living dead, waiting there to greet you like a scene from your darkest nightmares. A tall, rather obese zombie takes you in its arms and holds you tight. Then its mouth comes down and bites into your face, tears a long piece of skin loose from your cheek.

The pain.

The revulsion.

The *horror*.

Soon enough, several sets of hands reach for you. Several mouths tear off their own pieces of flesh. At one point, one of the undead faces pressing in toward you looks familiar.

Mrs. Rinehart?

You did tell her you'd come back for her. Looks like you kept your word. At least there's one thing you can feel good about.

THE END

Ray Wallace

Escape from Zombie Island

———————————————→ ←———————————————

Walking all the way to the hotel through the rain does not appeal to you in the least. The more you think about it, you become increasingly convinced you're safer here anyway. The place has to be infested with zombies and howlers at this point considering it was pretty much ground zero for the whole outbreak to begin with. Who knows? Maybe someone—the police, the military, a roving band of well armed and kind hearted people—will come along and help you out of this mess. If not, you'll stay put until morning. With daylight, things can only get better. Although you'd feel a lot more comfortable waiting around until then if you had a weapon in case some zombies or howlers chance upon your hiding place.

After waiting another minute to make sure Mr. Carjacker is long gone, you open both the tailgate and the topper door and step out into the storm. Circling around to the truck's driver side door, you're relieved to find it unlocked. You slide the bench seat forward and look behind it, reach down and grab the tire iron held in place there by a metal clip. A nice, blunt object good for smacking someone—or some*thing*—upside the head in the event you're attacked. You push the seat back into its previous position, climb into the truck then close and lock the door. Using the old style handles, you crack both windows, let the night air circulate inside the cab. The bench seat definitely beats the hard surface of the truck bed in the comfort department. If you want to, you could actually get some sleep in here. Considering what you've been through, however, you'll probably stay up all night. To say you're a bit wired from the night's proceedings would be a bit of an understatement. With some of the things you've seen, a part of you wonders if you'll ever sleep again.

You sit and watch as the occasional vehicle goes by, wishing one of them would stop. You could always stand next to the road like Mr. Carjacker did, wave your arms in the hopes that someone will pull over.

Maybe in a little while.

Right now, all you want to do is sit here and relax, try to calm your nerves and think rationally about your situation, figure out exactly what you're going to do if no one comes along to rescue you by sunrise. You can feel the adrenaline rush that's kept you going

181

throughout most of the evening starting to wear off. Feeling a sudden urge to rest your eyes for a bit, you lie down across the bench seat, use your arms for a pillow.

Damn, that feels good.

And then, of course, you fall asleep.

By the time you wake, the world around you has gone silent. No more rain tapping on the roof. No more grumbling and roaring of thunder. You sit up and rub your eyes, take a long look through the windshield at the world outside. Yes, the storm has passed and the darkness appears to have lifted a bit in anticipation of the dawn.

It seems you've been asleep for several hours. You wonder if, in that time, the entire island has been overrun by the walking dead. No way to know for sure, of course. What you do know is the truck's interior has become rather hot and stuffy. Needing some fresh air, you grab the tire iron from where it fell down to the floor while you slept, open the driver's side door and step out into the fading night.

It's so quiet.

You find it easy to imagine you're the island's last living person. Although, if you survived this long, you assume others have too.

The road glistens with a thin coating of rainwater. A few minutes pass and not a single car goes by. Above, a few scattered clouds drift across the sky, the remnants of the storm which has finally, thankfully, headed out to sea. You walk along the side of the road, past the front of the truck. And before you even realize what you're doing, you keep on walking. After about fifteen minutes, a young woman wanders out from behind a stand of trees along the other side of the road. You quicken your pace, sure she's about to scream and give chase. She doesn't scream, though. Instead, she moans as she heads across the street toward you, the sound plainly audible in the surrounding silence, her left arm hanging awkwardly at her side, like the shoulder's been dislocated. You break into a jog and leave her behind quickly enough as you continue onward to the hotel.

After that, you see more of them.

Three zombies kneel in the median, picking at the bones of something you're glad you can't identify as you pass by them, never getting to within twenty feet of the gruesome scene. One of the zombies turns its head and watches you with its empty gaze. Neither

Escape from Zombie Island

he nor his two companions bother coming after you.

A little further along...

Movement behind the windows of a white sedan parked haphazardly at the side of the road captures your attention. An old man with an empty eye socket presses his face against the inside of the driver's side window, gnashing his teeth and clawing at the glass, looking like he would really like to get his hands on you. If only he could figure out how to open the door.

And still further along...

A shuttle van like the one in which you rode from the airport to the hotel sits near the median with a flat tire. As you walk by, a dead woman with no lower jaw exits the van. Two more of the undead creatures follow. You outdistance them easily enough, though. Throughout all of this, not a single car goes by. Maybe you are the last person left alive on this island after all.

The zombie population increases the closer you get to the hotel. But you don't encounter a single howler. Good news, considering how much harder they are to deal with than the walking corpses. After wondering at their absence, you decide anyone who could be infected already has been infected. There's no one left around here— besides yourself—who could be turned into a howler. Now only the zombies remain.

Dozens of them wander around the last stretch of road leading over to the hotel with even more of them crowding the roundabout in front of the building. While you stand there, maybe twenty yards from the hotel entrance, the dead folk all turn in your direction and make their way toward you. The collective sound of moaning drifts upon the morning breeze heavy with the scent of saltwater along with something a bit less pleasant. More zombies emerge from the hotel as you circle the roundabout then follow the walkway leading out to the beach, the very place where all the long night's insanity began.

Stepping onto the sand, you marvel once again at the beauty of all that blue water rolling in from the horizon. An ocean paradise ruined by the presence of the living dead. You can hear them, still moaning, as they follow you onto the beach. Then another sound catches your attention over that of the waves crashing up against the shore: A distant *boom...* followed by several more. In your mind's eye you see bombs dropping from the sky, unleashing violence and destruction upon the small city at the heart of the island. The sound grows progressively louder during the next minute or so before stopping completely. During that time, you turn and head south along the beach, your undead entourage trailing behind you.

An ambulance sits at the edge of the sand at least a dozen yards from the water, one of its doors hanging open, clearly abandoned. The crashed airplane is gone. Sometime during the night someone came and towed it away. Did the local police remove it? The Air Force? Easy to imagine them wanting to cover up their involvement in everything that happened here, to deny any responsibility. The very idea of it causes a dull rage to burn inside of you.

You pass by a section of sand near the water line that's been scorched black, a reminder of what transpired yesterday evening. Looking over your shoulder, you see the pack of zombies following a good thirty feet behind you. The corpses appear to be having a little difficulty with the beach's uneven footing. As you watch, one of them, a little old lady, stumbles and falls down. You avert your gaze, pretty certain you recognize her—*Mrs. Rinehart?*—but not wanting to know for sure.

Another minute of walking and the scenery changes a bit. Houses line the higher, more solid ground to your left, beachfront property with a magnificent view of the water. Next to one of the houses you see a boat tied with a length of rope to a metal pole planted in the ground. Since there's no one around—no one living, at least—you walk over to the boat, see the rope has been tied in a lazy knot, easily undone. Apparently, the owners weren't too concerned with anyone stealing it. Shaped like a canoe, the boat measures about seven feet long with a small stabilizer attached to either side of it. Inside, a paddle lies across the bottom. You waste little time dragging the boat across the sand, happy to discover it's lighter than it looks. The zombies continue their steady approach, much too slow, however, to catch you before you enter the water.

You push the boat through the waves rolling in toward the shore. When the water reaches your waist, you clamber into the boat and paddle with everything you've got. It's tough going at first as you make your way out past the breakers. You work up quite a sweat by the time you reach gentler water where you paddle at a more leisurely pace. Looking back toward the shore, you see all those

Escape from Zombie Island

zombies standing there, watching you go. If they could talk you imagine one of them would shout: *Please don't leave, we haven't had a chance to eat you yet.*

You continue paddling out toward the deeper ocean. All the while the sun climbs higher in the sky making you wish you'd brought some drinkable water with you. A bottle of sun screen would be nice too.

The sound of bombs exploding resumes then eventually dies out again. For a little while you see a pair of planes in the sky, tiny with distance, above the tops of the palm trees standing in thick rows along the shoreline. Speaking of which… The beach has to be a couple hundred feet away now. If only you could keep paddling to the mainland. But it's too far. The sun and the heat would get to you at some point. And you can only imagine the trouble you'd face if another one of those storms came along. No, as much as you don't want to you know you'll have to head back to the island eventually.

Unless…

You see movement out on the water near the northern end of the island.

A yacht!

At the moment its course runs perpendicular to yours, taking it further out to sea. You raise the paddle, waving it in the air, trying to get the attention of someone on board. Long, anxious seconds tick by before the yacht finally turns and begins to grow larger as it approaches. A feeling of relief washes over you. After ten minutes or so, the steady hum of the yacht's motor drops in pitch while the boat glides up next to you. It's big, shiny and white with gleaming silver railings along the deck. An elderly man in a white shirt and a captain's hat approaches the railing, leans over it and smiles down at you.

"Hello, there!"

Two women join him—one of them about his age, the other much younger. A young man also appears and tosses down a rope ladder. Without hesitation, you use it to climb aboard.

A short while later you find yourself standing at the railing, gazing out across the water toward the island, sipping from a cold, fruity drink, the kind with a tiny umbrella floating in it. Introductions have been made and you've learned that the young woman is the elderly couple's daughter, the young man her fiance. Yesterday afternoon, the four of them made the trip from the mainland, arriving just prior to sunset. They dropped anchor offshore where they rode the storm out. Throughout most of the night they sat below deck, listening to the radio as reports came in concerning the horrors that had been unleashed across the island.

The boat travels at top speed now, leaving the island ever further behind. Airplanes continue to circle high in the air, occasionally swooping down toward the treetops, like vultures over a fresh carcass. At this distance, the purring of the yacht's engine drowns out the explosions.

"A terrible thing." The elderly woman leans against the railing next to you. She wears a loose fitting, flowery dress and holds a drink of her own. "You're lucky you got out of there alive."

You can't argue with that. So instead you take another sip of your drink and watch as the island disappears beyond the horizon. Standing there, surrounded by the wide blue ocean, your memories of the night before have the quality of a dream to them. *More like a nightmare*. Almost as though none of it really happened. But you know it wasn't a dream at all. It really did happen. The plane crash... The howlers... The zombies... All of it. And somehow, some way, you managed to survive.

Congratulations!

You escaped from Zombie Island.

You have found the One Way Out.

THE END

ABOUT THE AUTHOR

Ray Wallace lives in the Tampa Bay area and is the author of *The Nameless*, *The Hell Season*, *Escape from Zombie City: A One Way Out Novel*, and the short story collection *Letting the Demons Out*. He also writes book reviews for chizine.com. You can find him online at www.raywallacefiction.com.

ABOUT THE ARTIST

Zach McCain is an internationally published artist, primarily known for his illustration and cover artwork in the horror and science fiction genres. His work ranges from book and magazine illustration to graphic design, album art, and RPG games. He resides in Texas near the Gulf Coast. Published work can be viewed at his website: www.zachmccain.com.

Made in the USA
Lexington, KY
22 January 2014